ALL SHOTS

A DOG LOVER'S MYSTERY

ALL SHOTS

SUSAN CONANT

THORNDIKE
CHIVERS

This Large Print edition is published by Thorndike Press, Waterville, Maine, USA and by BBC Audiobooks Ltd, Bath, England.

Thorndike Press is an imprint of The Gale Group.

Thorndike is a trademark and used herein under license.

Copyright © 2007 by Susan Conant.

The moral right of the author has been asserted.

The text of this Large Print edition is unabridged.

Other aspects of the book may vary from the original edition.

Set in 16 pt. Plantin.

LIBRARY OF CONGRESS CATALOGING-IN-PUBLICATION DATA

Conant, Susan, 1946–
    All shots : a dog lover's mystery / by Susan Conant.
      p. cm.
    ISBN-13: 978-1-4104-0413-8 (hardcover : alk. paper)
    ISBN-10: 1-4104-0413-7 (hardcover : alk. paper)
    1. Winter, Holly (Fictitious character) — Fiction. 2. Women dog owners
— Fiction. 3. Dog trainers — Fiction. 4. Cambridge (Mass.) — Fiction.
5. Large type books. I. Title.
PS3553.O4857A79 2008
813'.54—dc22
                                        2007042582

BRITISH LIBRARY CATALOGUING-IN-PUBLICATION DATA AVAILABLE

Published in 2008 in the U.S. by arrangement with The Berkley Publishing Group, a member of Penguin Group (USA) Inc. Published in 2008 in the U.K. by arrangement with the author.

U.K. Hardcover: 978 1 405 64396 2 (Chivers Large Print)
U.K. Softcover: 978 1 405 64397 9 (Camden Large Print)

Printed in the United States of America on permanent paper
10 9 8 7 6 5 4 3 2 1

To Lynne and Dan Anderson
in memory of their beloved Stocker,
Ch. Grey Czar's Blue Chip Stock
(December 31, 1993–August 2, 2006),
the perfect malamute.

ACKNOWLEDGMENTS

Many thanks to Alaskan malamute Benchmark Heart's Desire and to Heart's devoted breeder-owner-handler, Phyllis Hamilton, for appearing in this book. Special thanks to Phyllis for talking with me about blue malamutes. I am also grateful to the late Jim Hamilton and to his delightful blue malamute, Benchmark Excalibur, called Steely Dan. Thanks, too, to my own malamute, Django (Jazzland's Got That Swing); to his breeder, Cindy Neely; and to Roseann Mandell and Geoff Stern; and to Jean Berman, Jessica Fry, Loulie Kent, Pat Sullivan, Margherita Walker, Anya Wittenborg, Suzanne Wymelenberg, and Corinne Zipps.

CHAPTER 1

I returned home on that wet September afternoon to find in my driveway a Harley-Davidson Screamin' Eagle Ultra Classic Electra Glide, a luxury road machine with power, pizzazz, and personality. It was outfitted with a myriad of snazzy features and accessories: heat shields, footboards, hardbags, compartments, racks, carriers, and a heavily padded seat with backrests for both driver and passenger. The chrome and the silver and the black leather glistened in the mist. The beast had a tinted wind deflector for a forehead, a big headlight muzzle, and for eyes, smaller lamps so clear and alive that they almost seemed to return my gaze, thereby confirming my sense that the two of us, the Harley and I, had not simply met before but knew each other in some deep and even mystical way. My soul mates, you see, are Alaskan malamutes, the ultimate canine touring models, Heaven's

Devils, all power, pizzazz, and personality, the Screamin' Eagle Ultra Classic Electra Glides of purebred dogdom. Even so, what in Hells Angels was this vehicular malamute doing in my driveway?

My name is Holly Winter. I live at 256 Concord Avenue in Cambridge, Massachusetts. ZIP code: 02138; the *right* one, as it's said, presumably by virtue of being shared with the alma mater of Ted Kaczynski, whose name is intoned in awed tones around here not because he was the Unabomber but because he was a Harvard math major. After all, how much intelligence does it take to be a psychotic multiple murderer? But to graduate from Harvard with a degree in mathematics? *That* takes brains. Cambridge, my Cambridge.

The Harley had a Maine license plate. I grew up in God's Country, the beautiful state of Maine. My father and my step-mother lived there, but Buck and Gabrielle never left home without their dogs, so the bike definitely wasn't theirs. I ruled out my husband on the grounds that he, too, would never buy a vehicle that failed to provide room for his dogs. Besides, he was canoeing in the Boundary Waters of Minnesota. With him were two of our five dogs: Lady, his pointer, and India, his German shepherd bitch, *bitch* being a good, clean word in the dialect of the dog fancy, meaning, as it does, female, unless preceded by the words *son of a,* in which case it means the same thing in the dog world as it does everywhere else. So, as the owner of the Harley, Steve was out. A Harvard classmate of my cousin Leah's? A few Harvard students had motorcycles, the men presumably to show that Harvard men could be real men, too. And the women? In a few cases, maybe to prove the same thing. Leah, with her red-gold curls, would've looked even more spectacular than usual on the Harley, but she, too, would've rejected any mode of transport that excluded big dogs, and in any case, she was chronically broke.

So, when I let myself into the kitchen, I half expected to find Leah there with a classmate whose early and middle adolescence had been exclusively devoted to conforming to the highest expectations of the Harvard Admissions Committee and who was now staging a belated, if normal, adolescent rebellion by becoming the reincarnation of James Dean. My cousin was, however, nowhere in sight. Seated at my kitchen table was a big, tall, handsome man with strong features that made him look like Michelangelo's statue of Moses and thus

11

like Charlton Heston as Moses, too, but with the broad forehead, the oversized eye sockets, and the prominent nose of the marble version. The biker lacked the horns of Michelangelo's Moses, of course, and if he was playing Moses at all, it was a beardless Moses at age thirty or so, a Moses with dark curly hair. It's possible that my brilliant dogs discerned the resemblance. Having evidently cast themselves as the children of Israel stunned by the wondrous sight of the tablets, Rowdy and Kimi had prostrated themselves before the man, which is to say that they were on their backs with their white tummies exposed and their white snowshoe paws waving in the air. The pose ordinarily represents nothing more than a demand for a belly rub, but it's important never to underestimate Kimi, whose accomplishments in a previous existence probably include a degree in mathematics from that place down the street. In fact, my first thought about how the biker had entered my house was that Kimi had let him in. Impossible! It was, I feared, remotely possible that she had figured out how to open the back door, but I was sure that she hadn't learned to unlock it. My second thought was that the uninvited visitor — intruder? — had found the key that I kept hidden under one of the trash barrels. Equally impossible. Absolutely no one but me knew about it. Even Steve didn't know.

"Holly Winter?" the man asked. "Hope I didn't startle you."

"Not at all," I said. "I habitually walk into my house to find strange men in black rain gear dripping puddles onto the floor. The phenomenon bothered me at first, but I'm used to it now."

He rose and extended a big mitt of a hand. "Adam."

What came to mind was the palindrome: *Madam, I'm Adam.* It even put a nervous little smile on my face. "Madam, I'm Adam," I said as I shook his hand. "A palindromic visitor."

The dogs were now on their feet and had their dark almond-shaped eyes fixed on me. People who don't train dogs often say, "Don't your dogs love you! They watch you all the time." My dogs certainly do love me, but the adoring gaze that always returns to my face is a carefully trained behavior.

"The girl with the red hair told me to wait inside," the man said. "Out of the rain."

Leah. Who else? Who else would've given free run of my house to a strange man who'd arrived here on a motorcycle in the rain but who couldn't be expected to wait

13

outdoors?

"She left," he added. Rising to his feet, he said, "You have something for me."

My principal employer, *Dog's Life* magazine, does not send couriers to pick up my columns. Still, if I had anything whatever for anyone at all, it was bound to be something or other about . . .

"Something about dogs?" I asked. "About malamutes?"

"You haven't heard from Calvin?"

The Calvin I knew well was a miniature schnauzer. "There must be some misunderstanding," I said.

"Holly Winter," he said.

The dogs sensed my relief even before I let my breath out. "You're looking for the *other* Holly Winter," I said. "She lives in Cambridge, too. We've had mix-ups before. That's what this is about. You've got the wrong one."

As if I'd released them from an obedience exercise, Rowdy and Kimi stirred a little. Rowdy meandered to the big water bowl and drank. Just as casually, Kimi moved her eyes from my face to the back door. I often had the uncanny sense that she could read my mind, but at the moment, I was practically reading hers. Domestic dogs, having evolved with us, are hardwired to follow the

14

human gaze: they look where we're looking, and they check out objects of our attention. As if acting on my desire to show Adam the door, Kimi took a few steps toward it. I nearly laughed.

"I'll give you her address," I said. Internet addict that I am, I usually use Web directories, but there was an old phone book in a cabinet under the counter. I pulled it out, looked up the other Holly Winter, scribbled her address on a notepad, and handed Adam the slip of paper. "It's off Kirkland Street, a left turn off Kirkland. When you leave my driveway, turn right. You have to. It's one-way. And then turn right onto Concord Avenue. Follow it almost to Harvard Square. Just before the Square, you'll see the Cambridge Common on your left. After the Common, go left. Get in the middle lane and take the underpass. When you come out of the underpass, turn left and then turn right on Kirkland Street. Then watch the signs. It's a left turn."

Like Kimi, I stepped toward the door. Although Adam had done nothing that felt at all threatening, I wanted him out of the house, in part so that I could call Leah and let her know exactly what I thought of her rotten judgment.

Adam thanked me. I opened the door. As

he was leaving, he paused briefly. "What kind of dogs are these?"

"Alaskan malamutes," I said.

"They're beautiful."

"Thank you," I said. "And that's some motorcycle you have."

He smiled.

"It's a Harley," I said. "I know that. But —"

"It's a Screamin' Eagle Ultra Classic Electra Glide."

And that's how I found out what it was.

Only later did I realize that whereas I'd observed the Harley closely and learned its name, I'd been so startled to discover its rider in my kitchen and so angry at Leah for having let him in and having left him alone in my house that I'd learned almost nothing about him. Him. The Harley rider. The young Moses. The man looking for Holly Winter. Adam. I knew that he drove a Harley-Davidson Screamin' Eagle Ultra Classic Electra Glide with a Maine plate. And I didn't even know his last name.

Adam: precisely what I didn't know him from.

CHAPTER 2

As Holly Winter — the other Holly Winter
— an, pause, other Holly Winter — another
Holly Winter or, in retrospect, yet another
Holly Winter — is walking through Harvard
Yard toward Quincy Street, a loose dog
takes a break from Frisbee to run toward
her in what I would undoubtedly have
viewed as a friendly manner. To her disgust,
the dog not only reaches her but goes so far
as to deposit its saliva on her, which is to
say that the dog licks her hand.

Yes, what kind of dog? The first question
to spring eternal to my dog-hopeful mind
— a Finnish lapphund, a Nova Scotia duck
tolling retriever, a fascinating mix of let's
guess which wonderful breeds? — never
even begins to cross hers. She does not
know, she does not ask, she does not care.
Rather, once the dirty thing has gone away,
she fishes in her purse, extracts a little
sealed packet containing a moist towelette,

and uses it to decontaminate her hands, thus defending herself against the threat of bacterial, viral, and parasitic disease. Such an extreme reaction! The dog's tongue, after all, touched only one of her hands, yet she cleans both.

I am tempted to make the rebellious claim that I, in contrast, would have licked the fingers the dog had lapped. Not so. Or not quite so. But it's quite likely that I'd subsequently have fixed food for myself and happily eaten it without first washing my hands. As it's said, better after a dog than after a person. The adage, by the way, is one I've been accused of misinterpreting. Specifically, I've been informed that the point I'm missing concerns the filth of human beings, whose dirtiness is said to exceed even the extreme foulness of dogs. Nonsense! The correct and true point concerns the microbial and spiritual purity of dogs, which is to say, their biological, not to mention cosmic, superiority to human beings.

But Holly Winter would certainly disagree. The other Holly Winter, of course. An other. Another. Yet another.

CHAPTER 3

The moment Leah answered her cell phone, I said, "Now Leah, I'm going to be blunt with you. You can be very high-handed, and I'm used to it, but this time, you've gone too far. You do not — repeat, not — let total strangers into my house and then just leave them here. I do not expect to arrive home and find bikers sitting in my kitchen, and I don't like it, especially when you know perfectly well that Steve is away and Rita is away and I am alone in this house and —"

"There was only one biker," Leah said. "And the dogs were there."

All three were with me now in the fenced yard, where I was keeping an eye on them while using my cell. Steve was always comfortable letting all five dogs run together, but I was more cautious than he was. For one thing, if they ripped one another apart, I'd be unable to stitch them back together. Steve has a general veterinary practice, but he's an excellent surgeon. Not that either of us encourages dogfights. As a dog writer and dog trainer, I know a lot about preventing them, and one of my rules is to be exceptionally careful if two of the dogs are intact male malamutes. Intact: unaltered, not neutered, possessed of the full male apparatus required to enter a dog in conformation at an American Kennel Club show. But more about that topic later. In fact, soon. Rowdy and his handsome young son, Sammy, were both entered on Saturday.

"Sammy was in his crate," Leah continued, "but I left Rowdy and Kimi loose. And it was twelve thirty or one. Steve and Rita would've been at work, not that Rita would —"

Steve and I have the first two floors of the house. Rita, who is our friend as well as our tenant, rents the third-floor apartment. A clinical psychologist, she'd just left for a psychotherapy conference in Palm Springs, in other words, for a tax-deductible ten-day vacation. The conference itself didn't actually start until tomorrow, Friday, and it ended on Sunday, but Rita had decided to treat herself to a week at a spa after the meetings were over. Cambridge psychotherapists are big on the idea that self-indulgence enhances mental hygiene. For all I know, Rita deducts the cost of manicures, pedicures, and hair coloring as if they were psychiatric treatments needed to maintain her emotional well-being.

"Rita knows how to make phone calls, but you're right. She'd have been seeing patients, and it's probably a good thing she wasn't here because I'd have had to listen to her interpretation of the Harley."

"The Harley was cool."

"What did I just say? Rita would've been interested in its symbolic value."

"Come on. You thought it was cool, too."

"Okay, it was cool. And the guy, Adam, wasn't all that scary, but you still shouldn't have left him here. Leah, I am not a nervous type, but at the moment, I'm aware that Steve and Rita are away, okay?"

"I'm staying there tonight. And tomorrow night. We can't move in until Saturday."

This was Thursday, September 7. Leah had spent the summer working at Steve's clinic and living with us. She was beginning her senior year, and the prospect of having her leave Greater Boston was breaking my heart. And all because damned Harvard didn't have a school of veterinary medicine! But she was applying to Tufts, which is in North Grafton and only an hour or so away, and everyone thought that she had a good

21

chance of getting in.

"I haven't heard an apology yet," I said.

"According to you, what you're supposed to do about undesired behavior is ignore it. If you don't reinforce it, it goes away."

"The principle doesn't apply to egregious violations. And it doesn't apply to self-reinforcing —" I broke off when the phone rang indoors. "The other phone," I told Leah. "It might be Steve. Bye."

Feminism being the force that it is in Cambridge, I feel the need to explain that I did not habitually hang up on women on the off chance that the incoming call on another line was from a man. While Steve was in the wilds of northern Minnesota, he did, however, have priority. Cell phone coverage in the Boundary Waters was unreliable. I hate call-waiting and had disabled it on my cell, so he might have gotten a busy signal and dialed our regular number.

"Rowdy, with me! This way, buddy." Leaving Kimi in the yard with our third malamute, Sammy, the adult-sized baby of the family, I hustled Rowdy into the house with me. The answering machine had picked up. My own voice was asking the caller to leave a message. The tone sounded, and Betty Burley began to speak. I grabbed the phone. Betty, who is top dog in our local Alaskan

22

malamute rescue group, is practically a member of my family, not only because we do rescue together but because Betty is a second manifestation of my own Kimi. Let me explain that all three of my malamutes are dark gray and white, as is Betty's hair. Betty lacks the "full mask," as it's called, that distinguishes Kimi from Rowdy and Sammy, who have "open faces," all white, in contrast to Kimi's combination of black goggles around the eyes, a black cap, and a bar down the muzzle. But Betty's oneness with Kimi is not a matter of appearance; rather, Betty and Kimi represent a rare instance of two bodies simultaneously inhabited by the same spirit. Identical twins are two separate individuals who have genetically identical bodies. With Betty and Kimi, it's the reverse: inside, they're the same individual; the difference between them is strictly corporeal. Strong and intelligent, they value their own opinions above everyone else's and have exactly the same air of quiet authority. Also, they snatch food. My strongest evidence for their spiritual unity is the oneness of my response to them. For example, on a potentially embarrassing occasion when Betty was having lunch at my house and got up to fix herself a third sandwich, I broke into a sweat and almost into tears, exactly as if my greatest fear about Kimi were being realized, namely, that she'd figured out how to open the refrigerator door. It's a miracle that I didn't snap, "Leave it!" at Betty and escort her to Kimi's wire crate.

On this occasion, Betty was not in a position to steal food, of course. In fact, her call was about rescue. "There's a message on my machine, and I need you to handle it," she said. "It's about a lost dog in Cambridge. Not one of ours. A Siberian." Ours are, of course, Alaskan malamutes. In the dialect of dog fanciers, a Siberian husky is a *Siberian* rather than a *husky.* An Alaskan malamute, however, is not an *Alaskan* but a *malamute.* An *Alaskan husky* isn't a purebred but is a mix bred for sled dog racing, whereas a cross between a Siberian and a malamute is known in malamute circles as a *Siberian cross* and in Siberian circles as a *malamute cross,* or sometimes as a *malberian* or a *Sibermute.* "A woman named Francie," Betty said. Then she dictated a Cambridge number.

One of the rules for dealing with tough dogs is that if the dog demands something, then he definitely does not get it. Even so, I complied with what I chose to interpret as Betty's request. A woman answered. After

24

I'd introduced myself, explained that I was from malamute rescue, and verified that I'd reached Francie, she asked whether it was my dog that had escaped from Mellie's.

"No, I'm from malamute rescue," I said for the second time. "If you'll give me the details about the dog, maybe I can help."

She spoke with the genteel vowels of the gown side of the town-gown divide. "It's all terribly complicated." She paused. "Because of Mellie."

Feeling impatient, I said, "Let's start with what happened. A dog got loose. In Cambridge, I gather. When did this happen?"

"Oh, not all that long ago, but Mellie is so conscientious, and she takes everything so literally. So concretely, really. I can't imagine that she actually needs any sort of license or permit to do what she does, but she's frightened of the police, all authority figures, actually, although she's hardly going to be arrested for dog-sitting without a license, is she?"

"I'm wondering exactly how long the dog has been missing. Days? Hours?"

"Oh, hours. Today."

"Great. From Mellie's house?"

"Her yard, I should imagine."

Stop imagining! Give me facts! "And where does Mellie live?"

25

"A bit north of Rindge Avenue. She's a neighbor of mine."

Persistence yielded Mellie's address, but when I asked for her phone number, Francie insisted on explaining Mellie to me.

"Mellie is the sweetest person on earth," Francie said. "She has special needs. She has the mind of a child, really. But I think it's fair to say that she's a model for independent living. She lives in the house she grew up in."

"Alone?"

"People help her. Her parents died before they'd touched their retirement money, so there's some sort of little trust fund, and there's a man at the bank who helps. She has someone who deals with bills. Her priest helps out. We pitch in. I make sure that she sees her doctor. The dentist."

"And she does dog-sitting."

"Mellie just loves animals. She had a little dog that died a few months ago, and she takes dogs in. She walks dogs. Feeds people's cats. It's all very informal. But unfortunately, she saw something on television that scared her, something about a kennel. I don't know. That's why she won't call animal control about this husky."

"Who's the owner?"

"I have no idea."

"And what does the dog look like?"

"It's a husky. Gray."

Gray doesn't go without saying. Both Siberian huskies and Alaskan malamutes exhibit a wonderful variety of coat colors. Furthermore, the average person can't tell one breed from the other. In different circumstances, I'd probably have probed for information about the dog's breed, including eye color. Happiest words in malamute rescue: *blue eyes.* Siberians have blue eyes, brown eyes, or, in bieyed dogs, one eye of each color, whereas all malamutes have brown eyes, preferably dark brown, sometimes light brown or even hazel, but never blue. There are many other differences between the two breeds, but a blue-eyed dog is, as Betty had phrased it, not one of ours. I also didn't bother to ask Francie why it was malamute rescue she'd called. Because the general public confuses the two breeds, we sometimes get calls and e-mail about Siberians. Like most other breed rescue groups, we are chronically desperate for foster-care space, so we have to reserve it for malamutes, but if I don't have to come up with a foster-care slot, I'm always happy to do what I can to help with a Siberian or, for that matter, any other breed or mix.

"Male or female?" I asked.

"Female."

"I'll do what I can," I promised, "but I have to warn you that Siberian huskies love to run. The dog could be long gone by now. But maybe not."

"Thank you," Francie said. "I really appreciate it. Mellie is special. She is a pure soul."

After I hung up, I said, "Hey, Rowdy, I've got a fun job for you. You want to go find a pretty girl?"

And we did find a pretty girl, too. Or a once-pretty girl. But not the kind I meant.

CHAPTER 4

In a self-sacrificing act of husband preservation, I'd insisted that Steve and I trade vehicles for his trip to Minnesota. My newish Blazer was much more reliable than his old van. Because of his attachment to the rattletrap, I never called it that within his hearing, but a rattletrap was exactly what it was: every loose part rattled, and every part sounded loose. But it was perfectly set up for dogs. It easily held crates for our five dogs, and it had boxes, compartments, and hooks for leashes, harnesses, old towels, veterinary supplies, and other gear that Steve always wanted to have at hand. Because of Steve's loyalty to the rattletrap, I hadn't come right out and said, "Look, if you try to drive that collection of loosely attached auto parts to Minnesota and back, it's going to break down en route if we're lucky, and if we're unlucky, you and the dogs are going to die in an accident, so take my Blazer." On the contrary, I'd pleaded with him to let me have his van so that Rowdy, Sammy, and I could have charming and convenient transportation to the show they were entered in on September ninth. Never marry a dog trainer. We are sooooooo manipulative.

To avoid the traffic at Fresh Pond, I took Garden Street to Sherman Street to Rindge Avenue and then wound my way down a couple of narrow streets with small, closely spaced wood-frame houses until I found Mellie's address. On the way, I kept an eye out for the loose Siberian but saw no sign of any off-leash dogs at all. Mellie's house was a tiny two-story place, a cottage, I suppose, painted pale green. It had a miniature front porch set so close to the street that the wooden steps ran almost to the sidewalk. On either side of the steps was a patch of well-tended lawn. I hate trying to parallel park the van, and there were no big spaces nearby, anyway, so I pulled into the empty driveway by the house.

When I got out, a short, slightly plump woman in a pink tracksuit came running down the sidewalk toward me. Her gait caught my dog watcher's eye: she rocked back and forth, and her step was heavy. Her age was hard to guess. Thirty? Thirty-five?

She had a round face, small brown eyes, and short brown hair. She looked vaguely familiar. Maybe I'd seen her in a local store or on the street. The drive from my house had taken under ten minutes, so it was likely that we shopped and walked in the same places. From Francie's description, I'd wondered whether Mellie might have Down syndrome, but her face showed none of the characteristic features.

When she reached me, she came to an abrupt halt, clutched the crucifix that hung around her neck, and said in a slightly hoarse, loud voice, "Did you find Strike?"

"No," I said, "but I'm going to try. I'm Holly. You must be Mellie."

After releasing the crucifix, she held out her hand with great formality. "Pleased to meet you."

When we shook hands, she seemed a bit unsure of when to let go, as if she felt a strong need to cling to something: her crucifix, my hand, anything. Letting go of her damp palm, I said, "No matter how careful you are, dogs get loose once in a while. With luck, the dog will come back on her own. Strike. That's her name?"

Mellie nodded and burst into tears. "I should've never left her alone in the yard! I only went into the house for like two seconds, and when I came out, she was gone. She went out under the fence. God is going to punish me!"

"No matter how careful you are, any dog can get loose. I'm sure that God won't punish you for being human. And I'm sure that God understands that Siberian huskies are escape artists. He'll take that into account."

Mellie's face was suddenly composed and serious. "Will He?"

"Yes. I'm certain of it. Now let's go over a few things. You were taking care of Strike. Is that right? That's her name?"

Mellie nodded.

"And she slipped out under your fence." I tried to keep the statement matter-of-fact. "The way dogs do," I added. "Now, when was that?"

Mellie rolled her eyes up as if the answer would be written in the heavens.

"Before breakfast? Before lunch? After lunch?"

Mellie nodded emphatically.

"After lunch?"

"Tuna fish," she said.

"So, after you had tuna for lunch?"

"Yeah. After." Her face clouded up. "You aren't going to tell the police, are you? Francie said you won't tell the police."

"No, there's no need to call the police. Strike hasn't been gone all that long. Besides, I have a good friend who's a policeman. If we do need —"

Mellie's face twisted in agony, and her hands became hard white fists. I'd intended to reassure her by telling her about my next-door neighbor, Kevin Dennehy, who is a detective rather than a finder of lost pets, but I decided against it. "But we won't need to," I said. "She may come back any minute. And we're going to look for her. I have lots of dog treats with me."

Mellie reached into a pocket and displayed a little pile of sliced hot dogs on her open palm. She had small hands with exceptionally short fingers.

"Perfect," I said. "And how does Strike feel about other dogs? Does she like other dogs? Not like them?"

With a sly grin, Mellie said, "She likes boys." To my relief, she went on to say, "But she had an operation."

"Excellent. I have one of my dogs with me. A boy. Rowdy. If Strike is still around here, she might be curious about him. Or he might help us find her."

When I emerged from the van with Rowdy on a six-foot leather leash, Mellie said solemnly, "Strike looks like that." After a pause, she added, "But different. Hi, Rowdy! Can I pat him?"

I gave permission, of course. Somewhat to my surprise, instead of thumping Rowdy on top of his head, Mellie moved to his side and gently touched his shoulder while murmuring, "Nice dog, nice big boy, Rowdy."

Big Boy responded by hurling himself to the ground, rolling onto his back, and presenting his white tummy. Mellie laughed like a child and then gave Rowdy the tummy rub he wanted. "All done for now, Mr. Rowdy," she said.

"Yes, all done," I echoed. "You're really good with dogs," I told Mellie.

Her face fell. "I was bad. I lost Strike. I —"

"We're going to look for her right now. Here's what I think we should do. You stay here, okay? In case she comes back. If you see any of your neighbors, tell them to watch for Strike. Ask them whether they've seen her. Ask children. Especially children. Kids notice dogs. If you see Strike, use your treats. Just hold out your hand with the food in it and walk toward your house door. Don't run after her."

"If you run after them, they run away."

"Exactly." I handed her a fabric slip lead

34

from Steve's clinic. "You know how to use this?"

With an expression of concentration, she passed the lead through the ring to make a loop.

"Perfect. If she gets close enough, just slip the loop over her head and tighten the leash. It's easier than grabbing her collar. Now Rowdy and I are going to check out the neighborhood, okay? And you're going to stay right near here. And call for her. Okay?"

Armed with treats of my own and a second slip lead, I set off. I kept Rowdy's lead loose and kept a close eye on him. Rowdy was not trained to track; his job right now was simply to be a lure for Strike. Still, I wanted to take advantage of the canine ability to hear sounds beyond the range perceptible to mere human beings, the miraculous canine power to detect scent, and my own skill in reading my dog. In between studying Rowdy for any change in his expressive face, the position of his ears and tail, or the quickness of his gait, I scanned for the lost dog, but neither Rowdy nor I picked up a hint of her presence. Our walk was an ordinary walk along city sidewalks paved in uneven brick, past wood-frame houses, many apparently built at the same time by the same builder, some gentrified, some not, many with porches, most set close to the street in a way that gave the area the cozy feeling of being a real neighborhood. A few blocks from Mellie's house, we ran into a couple of people, and I asked about a loose dog. One of them said he'd seen a husky about an hour ago. I tried calling Strike. Because of a lifetime devoted to dogs, I have a dog trainer's voice, by which I do not mean that I bark out commands; rather, when I speak to dogs, I expect them to understand and cooperate, and that's often what they do. "Strike!" I called. "Here, good girl! Strike!" My efforts entertained Rowdy, who waved his gorgeous white tail, pranced around, and conveyed his optimistic eagerness to have my happy expectations fulfilled by bursting into peals of *woo-woo-woo-woo-woo.* Rowdy, I might mention, is musically gifted. Kimi has a clear, true voice and excellent articulation, and Sammy *woo-woos* with force, but Rowdy's range and power are extraordinary. He is the Pavarotti of malamutes. Still, neither my calls nor his arias summoned Strike.

We headed back toward Mellie's. When we were four or five houses away, a young woman with braided hair and library pallor emerged from a doorway, and I asked whether she'd happened to notice a loose dog.

"Actually, I did," she said. "A big husky. Smaller than yours, but something like that. It went down a driveway. This was maybe thirty minutes ago."

"Near here?"

"I'll show you," she volunteered.

Rowdy and I trotted after her. When she was two doors from Mellie's, she stopped and said, "Here. The dog ran down that driveway. Good luck."

The woman walked away, and Rowdy and I headed down what was, in fact, a small cutout, a freshly graveled area with low shrubs on either side and exactly the space required for the one car that occupied it, a bright blue subcompact hybrid sedan. I remember wondering why the owner of the house hadn't sacrificed the greenery, widened the cutout, and rented out the parking space. In every possible way, Cambridge parking is a nightmare. Even if you have a resident permit for on-street parking, you're in danger of being ticketed and, worse, towed. In the winter, you have to be careful not to park in places that are tow zones during declared snow emergencies, and during the rest of the year, you have to check the signs to make sure that you aren't leaving your car on the side of a street scheduled for street cleaning. The towing for street cleaning is draconian: enforcement is vicious, and reclaiming your car is, as my neighbor Kevin Dennehy says, wicked expensive. Consequently, even the most unprepossessing little off-street parking space can go for a high rent.

The owner of this house, however, apparently didn't need the income. Like Mellie's, the place was almost a cottage, two stories high, with a small porch and wooden steps, but it had been recently painted in the warm yellow familiar from the Longfellow House on upscale Brattle Street. The windows looked new and had off-white fabric blinds, all lowered. When Rowdy and I walked to the end of the parking area, I saw that the backyard was landscaped with diminutive shrubs that I couldn't identify, a dwarf weeping tree of some sort, and a heavy layer of bark mulch. A five-foot-high wooden fence stained dark brown ran around the sides and the rear of the yard. There was no sign of the missing Siberian and no sign of anyone at home. Rowdy showed no particular interest in entering the yard. I continued mainly because the pale woman had said that the dog had been here. It was possible, I thought, that the owner of the pretty little house had taken her in and had perhaps called animal control. Only then did I realize that I'd neglected to ask Mellie whether Strike had an ID tag on her collar and, if so, whose name and phone number were on it. On second thought, would Mellie have noticed? Did Mellie know how to read?

When we rounded the corner of the house, I saw the full extent of the renovations. At the back were large sliding glass doors, and across the entire rear of the house ran a low deck with teak planter boxes, matching benches, and a small teak patio table and chairs. I also saw unmistakable evidence of recent neglect: the lawn needed mowing, and the petunias in the teak boxes were wilted, as were the mums and patio tomatoes in large terra-cotta pots on the deck. Cambridge being the temple to academe that it is, the life of the mind always has top priority around here; the failure to mow the lawn and water the plants might simply mean that the owner was writing the final chapter of a book or completing preparations to teach a new course. Still, I felt mildly critical. This yard was about the size of ours, and if we could miraculously cure the dogs of ruining our potential oasis of urban greenery, I'd find a few extra minutes every day to water the plants instead of letting them wilt.

When I stepped onto the deck and approached the glass doors, it was not, however, with the intention of delivering a lecture about horticultural responsibility. I merely wanted to take a close look at the planter boxes and the benches they supported, an attractive and sturdy set that I thought might stand a chance of surviving the dogs. No lights were on, and no sounds came from the house. Still, the bright blue subcompact was parked in the cutout. To avoid the embarrassment of being caught examining the furnishings on the deck, I made what I intended as the token gesture of rapping my knuckles on one of the glass doors. As I knocked, I looked in. Only a few feet from the glass door, on the tile floor of what proved to be a kitchen, a woman was sprawled facedown. Everywhere around her, in fact, everywhere I could see in the interior of the little house, were piles of broken crockery, cartons that had held milk and orange juice and cereal, emptied bags of flour and sugar, and books and magazines that had been tossed onto the floor. Potted plants had been knocked over. Next to the door was the carcass of a rotisserie chicken. Every cabinet door and every drawer was

40

open, as were the doors of the oven and the refrigerator. Two gigantic fish tanks must have been shoved off their low stands; the glass had been smashed and dead fish lay amid glass shards on the damp tile. The stench of rot and death must have leaked out around the door frame. The spoiled remains of the rotisserie chicken contributed to it, I'm sure, as did the heaps of damp food and the sad little tropical fish, but its principal source must have been the body of the woman and the blood that had pooled, congealed, and dried around her. She wore cropped white jeans now stained red and a bloodied aqua T-shirt that revealed what could only have been gunshot wounds. I froze in place and stared.

In books and movies, it's always the dog who alerts the dog walker to the presence of a corpse in a ditch or a shallow grave or under a pile of leaves and branches. Rowdy's only interest was in persuading me that we'd wasted enough time hanging around and that it was now my obligation to relieve his boredom. In other words, his contribution consisted of awakening me from my trance-like state of shock. When I turned from the scene of horror that lay inside, everything in the neat little yard and on the beautifully furnished deck seemed momentarily unreal, as if the handsome wooden fence, the weeping tree, the shrubs, the planters, and all the rest were nothing more than images cast by a projector. Then my eyes met Rowdy's, and his big, powerful, loving reality dragged me back to the world of substance. Sensing my disquiet, he moved to my left side, and I put my left hand on his back and leaned on him for support. The familiar texture of his coat, the coarse guard hairs over the soft padding of the undercoat, gave me comfort and strength, and his questioning look reminded me of the need to breathe and the need to take action.

"Dear God," I said aloud. "Rowdy, I love you with all my heart. Get me out of here."

CHAPTER 5

I stopped when we reached the sidewalk and then led Rowdy to the front of the house, where I found the street number on a decorative tile mounted next to the door. After taking a seat on the steps, I called 911 from my cell. Having promised to stay where I was, I remained there and tried to compose myself. My thoughts were racing. Mellie's fear of the police meant that the sirens would frighten her. For all I knew, she'd assume that I'd called the police to come and arrest her for dog-sitting without a license. But I couldn't go to her; I had to stay where I was until the police arrived and until I'd directed them to the deck, the glass door, and what lay beyond. The woman simply had to be dead. The scene had looked anything but fresh. The frames of the shattered aquariums were large. Those big tanks must have held a lot of water, but there had been no pools on the floor; all that remained was the dampness visible in the mess of flour, sugar, cereal, and whatever other food had been thrown to the tiles. Or was there a slight chance that the woman was still alive? Could anyone have lost so much blood and survived for the time it had taken the water to run off or evaporate? The petunias in the planters and the mums and tomatoes in the pots were so thoroughly wilted that the rain we'd had earlier in the day had failed to revive them. How long had it taken the plants to dry out so completely? Days rather than hours, certainly, but I had no idea how many days. Still, days rather than weeks. Wilted though they were, the plants were still green and still recognizable as petunias, mums, and tomatoes; they hadn't become anonymous brown stalks.

But Mellie! Should I run to her house and explain? Persuade her to follow me back here so she wouldn't be alone when the police arrived? There'd be an ambulance, too, and other emergency vehicles.

"And how do I *explain* to her?" I asked Rowdy. "We're two houses from Mellie's. Mellie probably knows her. And, of course, there's Strike, too, and Strike's owner, whoever that is. I have to find out. For all we know, Strike ran off and headed for home."

44

When the emergency vehicles approached, Rowdy's eyes lit up, and he began to raise his head. Before he had the chance to burst forth with glorious howls, I put a finger to my lips and said, "Shhh! Not more malamutes, buddy. Just sirens. Good boy."

A cruiser arrived first, and just behind it was an emergency medical van. Instead of wasting time searching for parking spots, the cops and the EMTs halted in the middle of the street, which was so narrow that it should probably have been one-way. I rose and rapidly explained to the older of the two cops, a massive guy with thick black hair, that I'd been looking for a lost dog when I'd happened to glance inside the door and had seen . . . but he should look for himself. Followed by the cops and two EMTs, Rowdy and I led the way to the backyard, where I pointed to the deck and the sliding glass doors. "In there," I said. "I'll be in front of the house."

No one objected, but the second cop accompanied us. He was a young African-American guy with light skin, hazel eyes, and the lean build of a long-distance runner. When we reached the graveled cutout, he leaned against the bright blue car and pulled out a notebook and pen. "Looking for a dog," he said. "Yours?"

"No. Just helping someone else." It's been pointed out to me that when I talk about dogs, I have a tendency to elaborate a bit. This time, I did not. Rather, I limited myself to giving my name, address, and phone number and saying that I had no idea who lived in the house. If I hadn't been so concerned about Mellie's reaction to the arrival of the police and, inevitably, to the news of a murder so close to home, I'd probably have mentioned Lt. Kevin Dennehy and said that he was my next-door neighbor. In fact, friendly person that I am, I'd have made some sort of contact with the young cop. Strangely enough, Rowdy took his cue from me. Instead of stacking himself in a show pose or demonstrating the full range of northern breed vocalizations or hurling himself to the ground to beg for a tummy rub, he made none of his usual bids for attention and admiration, but sat quietly and unobtrusively at my side.

In almost no time, I was free to return to Mellie's, as I promptly did. One glance told me that she was as frightened as I'd feared. In fact, she'd taken refuge inside her house. Still clutching the fabric lead, she was peering out through a front window. Catching sight of Rowdy and me, she opened the door, and before she had a chance to speak,

I said, "Someone needed an ambulance. That's why the police are here. It has nothing to do with you. You don't need to worry. But I didn't have any luck finding Strike."

Mellie shook her head back and forth. "Me neither."

"I have some ideas about what to do next." Instead of explicitly inviting myself in, I asked, "Is there somewhere we can talk?"

Mellie looked bewildered. From her point of view, I realized, we were already talking, weren't we?

"We could sit here on the porch," I said. It had two folding aluminum lawn chairs, the uncomfortable kind that find their principal use around here after snowstorms, when people who shovel out their cars are careful to designate the snow-free spaces as personal property rather than as the open-to-anyone spots on city streets that they might otherwise appear to be. Traffic cones and trash barrels are also popular choices. As a dog person, I take a keen interest in this local custom, which is clearly a human version of territorial marking, which is to say, leg lifting.

This time, Mellie got the point and invited me in. The first floor had only two rooms, a living room at the front, with a flight of stairs leading up to the second floor, and a kitchen and dining area at the back. The living room had brown carpeting, a brown couch, two brown chairs, a profusion of small pillows in bright colors, a large television set, and a great many small tables crammed with religious objects and framed photographs. On the wall hung two large reproductions of oil paintings, one of the Last Supper, the other of the Madonna and Child. The kitchen had dark brown cabinets and a floor of dark brown linoleum, but on the table in the dining area was a bright yellow tablecloth, and the refrigerator was plastered with photos of dogs held on by magnets. The little rooms were incredibly clean. The sink and appliances were white and unstained. Even the refrigerator magnets looked as if they'd been scrubbed. Francie had described Mellie as a model for independent living. I'd begun to wonder about the accuracy of the claim, but the sight of the well-kept house relieved some of my concern, as did Mellie's pleasant, ordinary offer of coffee and her obvious competence in using her coffee machine and in setting out mugs, spoons, a sugar bowl, and a pitcher of half-and-half.

As the coffee dripped, she showed me the

photos on the fridge. "My dogs," she said with a giggle.

"Dogs you take care of?"

"Rusty, I walk him. He's a Yorkie. Celeste. She stays with me sometimes." Most of the dogs were small or medium size, but there were a couple of Labs and a golden retriever. The highbrow names of some of the dogs gave Mellie trouble. The Pomeranian she called Kink and Guard was clearly Kierkegaard, but I was unable to translate a few of the others. To my amazement, she pointed to a picture of one of the Labs and said, "Milton has hip dysplasia."

Why shouldn't Mellie have known the term? What right did I have to be surprised? But I was. When she'd finished reciting the names of all the dogs, she addressed Rowdy, who was still on leash. "And you're a good dog, too," she said. "Rowdy, you want a cookie?"

Instead of pinching the treat between her fingers to offer it to him, she placed it on her flat palm, and when he scoured her whole hand with his tongue, she laughed so raucously that a tense dog might have been startled. Then she clapped the same moist hand over her mouth. "Bad! Be quiet!" In a near whisper, she said, "Good dog."

"Mellie, as long as you sound happy, he

doesn't mind if you laugh. Or even if you yell."

"Don't yell!" she protested in a near yell before adding softly, as if repeating an oft-repeated phrase, "Pretty voice."

Someone had obviously tried to teach Mellie to modulate her voice. A special education teacher? A speech therapist? Interestingly, although she sometimes lost control of her volume and had changed an unfamiliar name to familiar words, she'd mastered *hip dysplasia* and, even more strikingly, had used the dog trainer's term *cookie* in place of *dog biscuit*.

When we were seated at the table drinking our coffee, I reluctantly raised the topic of Strike. "Mellie, it's possible that she's gone home. Where is that?"

"Here."

"But when she isn't here. She's staying with you, but she belongs to someone else. Who is her owner?"

Mellie's face shut down.

"It's one thing if your own dog gets loose," I said, "but when it's someone else's dog? It's easy to feel really guilty about that, even though it's not your fault." For all I knew, Strike's escape was Mellie's fault, of course, but I had no intention of saying so.

Mellie's jaw was locked.

"This probably isn't the first time Strike has escaped from somewhere. Siberian huskies are escape artists. Some of them climb fences. They squeeze out under fences. Strike's owner has probably been through this before. Does Strike live near here?" Feeling increasingly like an interrogator, I continued to press Mellie. How long had Strike been with Mellie? Awhile. Was her owner a man or a woman? A girl. A nice girl. Yes, Strike was wearing a collar.

"With tags?" I made the mistake of calling Rowdy to me and showing Mellie the ID attached to his rolled leather collar. "Like these?"

"Like Rowdy," she agreed.

I had the frustrating impression that she was responding mainly to my suggestion; in reality, Strike might or might not have been wearing tags.

The only other piece of information I elicited was that Strike had arrived sometime after August 24, and I got that date by accident. Having abandoned my direct questioning about Strike, I gently asked Mellie about her own dog. Mellie produced a sheaf of snapshots that showed an adorable Boston terrier. Her name was Lily, and Mellie went on and on about her. Lily, I learned, had lived to fifteen and had gone to heaven. Father McArdle had said so. Mellie then produced a card with a picture of the Virgin Mary. In clear script, someone had written Lily's name on it, together with the dates of her birth and death. Lily had died on August 24.

"Were Lily and Strike friends?" I asked. "Did they play together?"

Mellie looked confused. Then, having apparently decided that I'd said something silly, she declared with a hint of scorn, "Lily was in heaven."

"So Lily went to heaven, and then, after that, Strike got here."

Mellie's response was loud and emphatic: "Of course!"

I gave up. Mellie and I then took a look at her backyard, which had a five-foot-high chain-link fence and a chain-link gate secured with a snap bolt. Either the missing Strike or another dog, perhaps many others, had dug holes in what remained of the grass, but some forsythia and a mock orange tree had survived. Visible at the rear of the fence was evidence of Strike's means of escape. The earth by the fence showed the signs of recent digging. Right under the fence itself was a small depression.

"Under and out," I said.

Mellie repeated the phrase.

"When we find Strike, I'll fix this for you," I promised.

Before Rowdy and I left, I wrote my name and phone number on a pad of paper next to Mellie's phone. Whether or not she could read, the information was worth leaving. Mellie had people to help her, and one of them would presumably read my number for her if she needed to call me. We agreed that she'd let me know immediately if Strike returned. I promised to do what I could to find the missing Siberian.

Pulling out of Mellie's driveway, I saw that the official vehicles no longer blocked the street. A small group of people had gathered on the sidewalk, but I had no desire even to pass by and drove in the other direction. Preoccupied with Mellie, I'd managed to blot out the image of the body on the tiles. It now returned to me. She had had my slim build. Her hair had been medium length, its color a pale brown with maybe a hint of red, a familiar shade, one that occurs in golden retrievers. Or so my father has always insisted. It is, in other words, the color of my own hair.

CHAPTER 6

As soon as I got home, I called Francie to tell her about the murder and to inquire about Mellie's safety. Our conversation was brief. "Mellie won't open the door to strangers, if that's what you're worried about," Francie assured me. "And she has good locks. Once Mellie masters a routine, she follows it. She always locks up. I'll break the news to her about what happened. She won't see it on the news. She watches TV, but mainly sitcoms and children's shows, a few animal programs, and she doesn't listen to the radio. Or read the newspaper, of course. News upsets her. Well, it upsets me, too. She can read, sort of, but she doesn't. I mean, she can print her name, and she can read words on signs and packages, stuff like that, but that's it. I wondered whether she might like reading children's books, but I tried a few, and I got nowhere. I'm sure she had unhappy experiences in school. The printed word makes her feel inadequate. In any case, one of us can always stay there tonight. Sorry, but I have to run." Her tone suggested urgency. "Our preschool is a media-free zone, and one of the toddlers keeps showing up in a Thomas the Tank Engine T-shirt."

Cambridge. It's worse than D.C. — one political crisis after another. Just let Thomas the Tank Engine chug his media-laden way across the city limits, and we'll face inevitable assault by the armies of Batman, Superman, the Power Rangers, the entire cast of *Toy Story,* and that notorious anti-feminist empress herself, Barbie, who'll wear either her Joan of Arc outfit or her cute little U.S. Marines uniform, but will waste precious hours deciding between the two, thus giving us time to erect our fortifications of anatomically correct and racially unidentifiable dolls, unembellished blocks, Lincoln Logs, LEGOs, unpainted wooden trains, jars of finger paint, pads of blank paper, and other toys designed to challenge the imagination, boost IQs, and instill in our children the extreme tolerance for unrelenting boredom so vital to success in today's academic world.

It was now quarter of five. I placed quick calls to the animal control officers of Cambridge, Arlington, Somerville, and Belmont, on all of whose voice mail I left my name, my phone number, and the message that a female Siberian husky had been lost near Rindge Avenue in Cambridge. Since Strike had been missing for only a short time, it was premature, I decided, to post flyers and to enlist the aid of the world's greatest finder of lost dogs, the Internet. As we say here in Cambridge, think globally, act locally.

Instead of cooking, I ran down the street to Formaggio, a gourmet shop principally renowned for delicious cheeses from all over the world but also notable for fruits, vegetables, and flowers and for rotisserie chicken that has the distinction of not tasting like those freeze-dried poultry strips sold as dog treats. I arrived home to find Kevin Dennehy at my back door. For a person with red hair, blue eyes, fair skin, freckles, and a friendly manner, he is remarkably reminiscent of a silver-back male gorilla. He has the same massive build, including the muscular shoulders, and he sometimes lets his arms swing down as if he were contemplating quadrupedal locomotion, but the main point of likeness is Kevin's peculiar ability to combine an air of authority with an attitude of curiosity. Kevin would strangle me for describing him as cute, but cute he can be.

To my amazement, Kevin skipped his usual formulaic greeting ("Hey, Holly, how ya doing?") and said, "Christ, am I glad to see you. I thought you were dead."

"Reports were greatly exaggerated," I said. "Kevin, I have to feed the dogs, and then I have dog training, but if you're hungry, I've got chicken that I'll be glad to share."

Five minutes later, Kevin was seated at my kitchen table with a can of Bud in front of him and his massive hands clamped over his ears. As I've said, he's cute. The gesture was, however, practical and justified: I was feeding Rowdy, Kimi, and Sammy, which is to say, three exemplary specimens of the most stunningly beautiful, inventively brilliant, and passionately food-driven breed ever to set gorgeous snowshoe paw on the fortunate planet Earth. Rowdy and Kimi were hitched to doors at opposite ends of the kitchen, Sammy was in a wire crate, I was dribbling safflower oil onto a combination of Eagle Pack and EVO in three stainless steel bowls, and all three dogs were screaming, screeching, hollering, bellowing, and bouncing up and down as if their last meal had been weeks ago instead of a mere ten hours earlier. Ages ago, I'd read the report of a small study that compared the behavior of malamute puppies and wolf cubs. Whereas the little wolves showed a healthy interest in meals, the baby malamutes went nuts around the food dish. That's my paraphrase, of course, but the point is that instead of saying that voracious eaters wolf down dinner, we really ought to say that they malamute it down. Anyway, to show my understanding and respect for the pack hierarchy, I fed Rowdy first, then Kimi, then Sammy. By the time Kimi's bowl hit the floor, Rowdy was flat on his belly with his dish gripped between his front paws and his face in his dinner, and by the time I'd slipped Sammy's food into his crate and shut its door, Rowdy's bowl was empty. To someone accustomed to normal dogs, malamute mealtimes can be a shock, but Kevin was used to the madness, which was over in almost no time.

I then let Rowdy and Kimi out into the yard, let Sammy out of his crate, and joined Kevin at the table. "What must've happened," I said, "was that someone confused the name of that poor woman with the name of the person who found the body. Me. Holly Winter. I'm sorry you thought —"

"It wasn't that," Kevin said. "It was the ID."

"The *other* Holly Winter. So that's who it is! The poor woman! Kevin, what a weird coincidence. Actually, it's the second one today. The second mix-up. This is freakish. Some guy on a motorcycle was here looking for her. No wonder he was having trouble finding her. Now I know why."

Kevin said, "I thought you didn't believe in coincidence."

"I don't." I paused. "Usually."

The theory is that behind every so-called coincidence lies a series of connections, some small, some large, that, if traced back far enough, lead inevitably to the great source of meaning and purpose in this otherwise senseless universe, namely, dogs. As a theory, this one may not initially seem to be right up there with relativity, for example, or evolution by means of natural selection, but I have seen its predictive value demonstrated countless times throughout my life and thus should have known better than to append that foolish *usually.*

"I knew she lived in Cambridge," I said. "The other Holly Winter. Kevin, this is so horrible. I wandered back there, behind that house, looking for someone's lost dog, and when I saw . . . it was sickening. Her body was right by the door, just on the other side of the glass door. Everything had been thrown around. Anyway, when this biker was here, I looked up her address for him, but it was off Kirkland Street. She must've moved. I used an old phone book. I've never met her, but I know a little bit about her. We had the same doctor for a while, and one time I called, and the doctor said, 'Well, well, how's the bladder infection?' I didn't have one. She did. She had something to do with Harvard — a graduate student or a lecturer or something like that. I am so sorry!"

"It isn't her house," Kevin said. "It looks like she was house-sitting. There's a suitcase and some clothes in one of the bedrooms. And long lists about taking care of tropical fish. Instructions."

"The tanks had been broken. Knocked over."

"Some of them. There's more all over the place."

"Whose house is it?"

"A doctor. Young guy. Dr. Ho. He's in Africa with some kind of medical group."

"This is going to sound irrelevant, but do you happen to know a woman named Mellie who lives right near there? Two houses away."

Kevin grew up in Cambridge and knows half the city. "Mellie O'Leary." He smiled. "My mother knows her. Knew her parents."

"Mellie is the reason I was there. She was taking care of someone's Siberian. The dog got loose, and I was trying to help. I'm not supposed to have told you that, by the way. Mellie is terrified of the police. She does pet-sitting, dog walking, in a minor way, and she thinks she'll get arrested for not having a license. Anyway, Mellie is the reason I was there. She was taking care of a dog that got loose. But the point is . . . Mellie is . . . I guess the word is simpleminded. The woman who called me about helping to find the dog says that Mellie locks up and that the neighbors watch out for her, but is she okay there? She lives alone, and it's only two houses away. Was this murder, uh, personal? Or . . . ?"

"Looks like a search for something. Probably something small. This Dr. Ho's got a good sound system, and that wasn't touched. New computer's there. He's a whatchamacallit, social justice type, believes in simple living. It wasn't some junkie who'd've grabbed anything."

I nodded. "I saw the food on the floor. Things that had been dumped. So, are you assuming that he thought the house was empty and that Holly Winter surprised him? While he was searching for something."

Kevin shrugged. "Hey, don't ask me. I just found out it wasn't you."

Over our hurried dinner of rotisserie chicken, I tried to pump Kevin for additional information, but if Kevin knew more, he wasn't saying it.

CHAPTER 7

Unbeknownst to me, the other Holly Winter, she who once had a bladder infection, far from having been shot to death while fish-sitting for Dr. Ho, still lives — and still lives where I thought she did, off Kirkland Street. The address had made me imagine her in grand surroundings. Julia Child's kitchen, now in the Smithsonian, was dismantled and removed from a house in that neighborhood. The late John Kenneth Galbraith, author of *The Affluent Society,* lived there. How convenient for him! To study personal wealth in American society, he merely had to stroll around the block.

But Holly Winter, this other Holly Winter, does not occupy one of the grand old places. Elsewhere she might be said to rent a garage apartment, but since her abode is a short walk from the academic center of the American universe, which is to say, anywhere but *elsewhere,* she lives on the second floor of a renovated carriage house. Or does she? After a summer in England, she refers to the second story of the not-a-garage as the first floor and takes care never to say *apartment* when *flat* can be put to use.

Her taste is minimalist: simple blinds, no curtains, sleek black couch and chairs, no throw pillows, black filing cabinets, no piles of paper, hardwood floors, no rugs, hundreds of books neatly aligned on bookshelves, no paintings, no prints, no pieces of sculpture, no photographs, certainly no snapshots, and nothing even remotely like geegaws or tchotchkes. She now sits at her teak desk, its surface clear except for her notebook computer, the screen of which displays a document she is drafting for the CAMP, the Cambridge Alliance for Media-free Preschools, an organization that she has recently begun to support by serving on the group's advisory board. To her annoyance, instead of merely being asked to advise, she has been asked to contribute by analyzing data from a study intended to evaluate the impact of a media-free policy on children in participating preschools and day-care centers. As is invariably the case with projects inspired and implemented by idealistic reformer-educators, the design of the so-called study is a mess, principally because the statistician, Holly Winter, this Holly Winter, was called in only after the data had been collected. Even so, she approves of CAMP's goals. Surely the world is improved by stripping away this ghastly media trash and giving the imagination free rein! Also, she approves of the membership of the CAMP Advisory Board, including as it does Zach Ho, a Harvard classmate of hers, a man with just the sort of keen intelligence that attracts her most.

CHAPTER 8

The Cambridge Dog Training Club meets at the Cambridge Armory, which is on Concord Avenue near the Fresh Pond rotary. The club serves a wide area, but a fair number of Cantabrigians attend classes, so I decided to ask around to see whether anyone knew Mellie. Instead of training one of my own dogs, I worked at the desk as people checked in. Then I helped to teach the puppy kindergarten and the beginners' class. Since this was the first Thursday after Labor Day, it was the first night of training after the summer break. The desk was busy because of all the new people signing up and paying, so I felt useful. I put a little notice about Strike on the desk, but no one responded to it. The classes weren't as much fun as you might imagine because the club asks handlers to leave the puppies and the beginner dogs at home for the first meeting. The first day of school can be as exciting and stressful for dogs as it is for children, but dogs, of course, respond by barking, and if they're present, it can be almost impossible to communicate basic information to the handlers. Still, I had a good time and even managed to find a couple of people who knew Mellie. Both of them said that she was a sweet person who genuinely loved animals and who did some informal pet-sitting, dog walking, and boarding. One of the people knew Mellie from St. Peter's Parish, which is a Roman Catholic church on Concord Avenue, a few blocks from my house as you head toward Harvard Square. It seemed to me that there had to be a church closer to Mellie's house than St. Peter's, but when I said just that, I learned that although Mellie sometimes attended Mass elsewhere, she remained a regular at St. Peter's, in part because she was used to it, and in part because one of the priests there, Father McArdle, had promised her parents that he'd look out for her and had kept his promise. Mellie, I remembered, had mentioned the name.

I got home to find a message from Steve on the machine. "I know you're at dog training," he said in that deep, calm voice I adore, "but my cell's not working much here, and I managed to get through, so I thought I'd tell you that we're okay. We're fine. We're great. I love you." My effort to return the call was useless, but I did leave a message. I said nothing about the murder. If Steve knew that a woman named Holly Winter had been shot to death in Cambridge, he'd inevitably worry. He worked tremendously hard and deserved this vacation. I'd tell him everything when he got home.

I could not, of course, protect myself from knowledge of the murder, but the remembered sound of Steve's voice soothed me to sleep, as did the thought that Leah would return in an hour or two and that I wouldn't be alone in the house. Not that I was. All three dogs were in the bedroom with me, Sammy in his crate, Kimi the bed hog jammed next to me, and my ever-hopeful Rowdy curled up on the floor beneath the silent air conditioner. In the morning, I awakened with the thought that Holly Winter wasn't all that unusual a name and that people with really popular names must get used to having their namesakes murdered all the time. If I were Mary Kelly or Lisa Johnson, it would still have been eerie to come upon the body of a woman with the same name, much weirder than merely reading about her death in the newspaper, but the principle was identical, and meaningless coincidences did occur, that is, coincidences that were just that and not dog-meaningful reminders to hunt for hidden patterns and obscure interconnections. Furthermore, I had a busy day and, indeed, a busy weekend ahead, with no time to reread Conrad's *The Secret Sharer* or otherwise to dwell on the creepy matter of doppelgangers.

By the time Leah got up, I had fed the dogs, done my morning chores, taken a shower, and called Mellie. Strike had not returned. Consequently, I'd posted messages about her to all of my malamute e-mail lists and the lists for dog writers, with the request that my posts be forwarded to other lists. I'd also prepared and printed copies of a lost-dog flyer that gave my phone number and promised a reward. Leah got up at nine and arrived in the kitchen with her curly red-gold hair damp from the shower and piled on top of her head in a sort of bohemian beehive. She looked perfectly lovely and entirely innocent of such crimes as giving Harley-riding strangers the run of my house. I toasted an English muffin for her and gave her a cup of coffee. Then I told her about the previous day.

"You were looking for a lost dog and you found a dead body?"

"Bodies are dead bodies," I said.

"And her name was Holly Winter? That's . . . after the guy on the Harley was looking for her?"

"I told Kevin about that. But she'd been dead for . . . I don't know. Days, I think. The biker couldn't have left here and then murdered her. And it really has nothing to do with me. I'll know more tonight. Kevin and I are having dinner. Until then, I'm just going to stay busy. I'm taking Rowdy and Sammy to the LaundroMutt. They're both entered tomorrow. After the show, Buck and Gabrielle are coming back here. They're staying here Saturday night."

"Lucky you."

"Leah, really! I love having Gabrielle here, and she's pretty good at keeping a lid on my father. And at least Steve is away, so I don't have to try to keep Buck from grating on his nerves."

"Do you want me to stay? I was going to move out tomorrow, but I could stay another few days."

I'd have loved it. "No, of course not. But thank you. All your friends are coming back. You'll want to see them."

"If you change your mind . . ."

70

"I'll let you know."

"But I'm going to help you groom."

"You don't have to."

"The LaundroMutt is a cool place. I want to."

"I'd love it," I said.

An hour later, we were at the Laundro-Mutt, which is, as Leah had said, a cool place, a self-service dog wash on the Fresh Pond rotary. Leah had Sammy in one of the big stainless-steel tubs, and I had Rowdy in the one next to it. Sammy, I should note, is a funny malamute. For one thing, he loves to fetch balls. He'll keep retrieving as long as I keep throwing. Kimi regards this behavior as a sign of mental aberration. As Sammy flies after a ball and returns it to me, she watches him with an expression of perplexed disdain. For another thing, Sammy likes water. Kimi doesn't mind it and will even go swimming, but Rowdy hates water. What he detests is the sensation of water on his skin, especially on his belly. I'd had to lure him into the stainless-steel tub with a fistful of roast beef, and even using the treat, I'd had to shove him up the folding ramp to get him in. Now that he was hitched to the tub and soaking wet, he was behaving himself in the sense that he wasn't fighting to escape, but he was bellowing complaints

71

that must have been audible in Harvard Square. When the dogs were thoroughly rinsed, we used the big professional dryers to blow them dry. My latest grooming discovery, the Chris Christensen 27mm T-brush, did an admirable job of grabbing hair that would otherwise have flown all over the place, and the T-handle minimized wrist strain. Even so, by the time we finished, most of the air in the LaundroMutt had been displaced by malamute undercoat, which probably lined our lungs. Leah is a decent groomer, but I'm better with nail clippers and scissors than she is, so I cut the dogs' nails and then neatened their feet with a little trimming. Father and son looked spectacular, thus prompting me to check the sky for the black clouds that laborious show grooming generates. I swear that the harder I work on a dog's coat and the better he looks, the more likely it is that rain will pelt down and, worse, that in spite of extreme vigilance, the dog will somehow find a gigantic mud puddle and transfer its contents to his coat. The sky had not yet darkened. Not *yet.*

I posted one of the flyers at the Laundro-Mutt. When we got home, Leah left on her bike — her bicycle, of course, not a Harley or the like — with some flyers to post in the

Square, and I went to Loaves and Fishes for food shopping, made a beef stew to serve to Buck and Gabrielle the next evening, checked the guest room, and was just sitting down to squeeze in some work time when the phone rang.

"Francie here."

I was elated. "Has Strike turned up?"

"Sorry. No. No news at your end?"

"Nothing. I've posted to a lot of lists. That's the most effective thing to do. I've also started putting up flyers. The other thing would be to contact the owner and find out whether Strike headed for home, but when I asked about the owner, Mellie clammed up."

"I have no idea why. Mellie does do that, though."

"Maybe you could talk to her. She knows you, and she's just met me. Among other things, the owner has a right to know what's happened."

"It's possible that Mellie made some kind of promise. She takes promises seriously. And concretely. Her universe is very black and white."

"But why would she . . . ? Well, maybe. I guess it could be a divorce situation, a sort of custody battle, and one of the partners could've stashed the dog with Mellie. Would

73

you see if you can find out? See if you can get Mellie to say anything."

"I'll try, but I probably won't get anywhere, especially with Mellie so anxious. After what happened to Zach's house sitter."

"Is that Dr. Ho?"

"Lovely man. One of Mellie's mainstays. He's the one who gave her the DVD player and set it up for her. He somehow managed to make it so simple that she can use it. I wish someone would do that for me! And he tracked down all those DVDs about dogs."

"I wondered," I said. "She actually does know a lot about dogs. I wondered where she'd picked up the vocabulary."

"Well, that's where. She watches those things all the time. Some Scandinavian earth mother. I don't know."

"Turid Rugaas," I said. "Does Dr. Ho have a dog?"

"Fish. Except that the poor things are probably all dead now. That's why he had this house sitter, really. He'd've been better off hiring Mellie, but he knew she'd have trouble. Something about different tanks on different days, and if you overfeed them, they die. And the truth is, I think he was reluctant to give her the responsibility. Not that Mellie would've particularly wanted to be responsible, either, not for that long. Three weeks. And he's in Africa. It isn't as if he could come running home if there were problems."

"So, Holly Winter, the other one, was . . ."

"What?"

"That woman and I have the same name. It's very —"

"She's unidentified," Francie said.

"Are you sure? What about her car?"

"What car?"

"A little blue car. In the driveway. The parking space next to the house."

"That isn't hers. It's Zach's." Francie cleared her throat. "We think, uh, the neighbors think . . ." She paused. "Zach has a little weakness."

"For cars? That one didn't look —"

"No, not cars. He has an eye for the ladies, so to speak."

"He got one of his girlfriends to house-sit? I don't see that that's —"

"He hadn't necessarily known her for very long." Hesitantly, she added, "Meaning for more than a few hours. He, uh . . ."

"He picks up women," I said. "At bars? Clubs?"

Francie laughed. "Not at all! We think his favorite place is Loaves and Fishes. You know those tables at the front? He buys sushi and then . . .”

“He picks up women at a health food supermarket? That’s —”

“Zach is very attractive. Charming. Very appealing. Why he . . . well, I have no idea. But he does.”

“Maybe he likes his women well nourished,” I said.

After a moment’s silence, Francie said, “I think I consider that a sexist remark.”

“Not at all. The preference must extend both ways. The women are presumably picking him up, too. For all we know, they lurk at the sushi counter and trail after him. Or it’s a process of perfect equality. The raw fish acts as an aphrodisiac on both sexes alike, and whatever happens after that is strictly between consenting adults.” I paused. “Unless, of course, one of them ends up dead.”

CHAPTER 9

Kevin Dennehy's gigantic appetite helps to account for his horrible taste in restaurants. He loves any place that dishes out mammoth portions. If he were served a plate heaped with garbage, he'd be perfectly happy as long as there was lots and lots of garbage, especially if it contained very few green vegetables. My dogs love vegetables, but life with malamutes has accustomed me to Kevin's general attitude. I have often thought that instead of training my dogs with liver, cheese, and beef, I could use eggshells and coffee grounds. The dogs would get sick, but before they did, they'd work as hard as they do now. Consequently, it's easy for me to resign myself to allowing Kevin to decide where we eat. The occasion has seldom arisen since he started going out with Jennifer Pasquarelli, whom he did not, I might mention, pick up over sushi at Loaves and Fishes. Still, she is exceptionally well nourished, at once buxom and trim. When they eat out, Jennifer drags Kevin to Asian restaurants and forces him to eat vegetables with foreign names. Jennifer is a Newton, Massachusetts, police officer, and she and Kevin met on the job. Actually, she was in trouble then because of her rude behavior to a Newton taxpayer, and Kevin was free this Friday night because she was in similar trouble once again. Specifically, when summoned to investigate a typical suburban crime, namely, the theft of a Mercedes-Benz hood ornament, Jennifer told the citizen to trade in his "goddamned status symbol" for a Ford or a Chevy and quit bothering the police about trivia. So, for at least the second time, Jennifer had been packed off to a training course on developing social skills for effective community law enforcement, and Kevin was free to pig out on meat.

The restaurant he selected was one of his better choices, by which I mean that it did not have the reputation of giving its patrons food poisoning. It was a chain eatery in a big converted warehouse. The interior space was barnlike. The decor was based on rough wood and dead animals — rustic beams, deer heads, moose heads, stuffed pheasants — but the booths were cozy, the service was friendly, and the menu was extensive. The offerings did not, oddly enough, include venison, mooseburgers, or game birds, but there wasn't an Asian dish among them, and the vegetarian items were in the pasta section and contained only what Kevin deems "normal" vegetables, that is, tomatoes and the like, and not bok choy, Chinese cabbage, or wild mushrooms. I ordered a Caesar salad and fettuccine Alfredo. Kevin went for a double portion of deep-fried mozzarella sticks to be followed by a sixteen-ounce steak with french fries. He was driving, so he had Coke instead of beer, but I had a glass of Merlot that wasn't half bad.

One of the appeals of the restaurant, from Kevin's viewpoint, was the fast service. The drinks had appeared immediately, and we'd barely ordered the food when the server returned with our appetizers. I took the arrival of my salad and Kevin's mozzarella sticks as a signal that he'd finally discuss the murder with me. On the way to dinner, he'd refused to say anything about it. His excuse had been that there were things he wanted me to look at, and when he'd parked his car, he'd retrieved a briefcase from the backseat and carried it in with him.

After devouring a mozzarella stick, he shifted his briefcase from the floor to the seat of the booth, pulled out a sheaf of papers, and placed them on the table. "These are photocopies," he said, as if to assure me that he hadn't broken any rules about absconding with evidence. It struck me that he looked less like a gorilla than usual. The briefcase was one source of the impression. Also, he was wearing a khaki suit, a white shirt, and a flowered tie in colors that picked up the red of his hair and freckles, and the blue of his eyes. Non-ape colors: khaki, red, blue. And from the front, you couldn't see that the suit jacket was stretched taut over his back and shoulders.

"Am I allowed to look at them?" I ate some romaine, which was covered with hard granules of cheese. "Right side up?"

"That's why I brought them."

"This is my phone bill. Electric bill. Bank statement. I keep meaning to tell the bank to stop sending paper statements. I do all my banking online. Where did you get these?" I should explain that when Steve and I got married, he moved in with me, I kept my original name, and I didn't bother to inform the utility companies of our union, so many of the household bills were addressed only to me. "What happened? The trash people rejected my recycling for some reason, and . . . ?" Cambridge trash and recycling regulations are fierce and are fiercely enforced. You can be ticketed for putting out improperly prepared recyclables. The city doesn't yet respond to violations of the trash rules by hauling away our bins and barrels, but I fully expect it to happen. But photocopying the offending papers and turning the matter over to the police? Too much even for Cambridge. "What's going on?"

Kevin was on his second plate of mozzarella sticks. He swallowed, wiped his hands, and again reached into the briefcase.

"Kevin, if you intend to show me one of those horrible death photos, I don't want to see it. I saw that poor woman once. That was more than enough." I ate a little salad and added, "But, okay, I didn't see her face. Apparently she's not the other Holly Winter. Someone told me she was unidentified. If you really need to know whether I recognize her, I can do it."

What the photograph showed wasn't a woman at all. I studied it closely. It was an eight-by-ten print with sharp focus and excellent detail.

"Tell me about him," Kevin said.

"Her. Female. I'm all but positive. She's a malamute. You knew that."

"I figured."

"She's a breeder dog. Show lines." *A breeder dog:* a dog from a reputable kennel rather than from a backyard breeder, a pet shop, or one of those ghastly Web sites that are nothing more than cyber pet shops. "Where did you get this?"

"All this stuff," Kevin said. "All of it was in Dr. Ho's house."

"My utility bills? And a picture of a blue malamute? That's what she is. Blue. The color is rare. It's the rarest malamute color. It's distinctive and unusual. I know she doesn't look sky blue, but that's what this color is called."

"Gray."

"This shade of gray is called blue. Like Russian blue cats, okay? It's called blue. Take a look at the pigment on her nose. In my dogs, it's black. Hers is slate gray. Or blueberry, except that it's more gray than blueberries really are. And her eyes are light. It's a little hard to see in the picture, but they're not the dark brown you're used to seeing. She's a blue malamute. I've never seen her before. And I'd remember. I've seen pictures of blue malamutes, but I've actually seen only a few of them. The first one I ever saw belonged to a really nice man named Jim Hamilton. Jim died a few years ago. His wife, Phyllis, is a top breeder, and she has blue in her lines. Anyway, Jim had a dog called Steely Dan, and at shows, people always wanted to see the blue malamute, and Jim was always good about going out of his way to —"

The server removed Kevin's empty plate, left my half-eaten salad, and presented us with our main courses. I belatedly realized that my fettuccine Alfredo would contain the same flavorless cheese granules that were in the salad, as proved to be the case, but melting had improved the cheese, and the pasta was less mushy than I expected. Kevin's steak looked big enough to feed six people. It was served on a platter and accompanied by a bushel or two of french fries.

"You want some?" he asked.

"Far be it from me to take food away from a growing boy. Anyway, this is a blue malamute, but I don't think that Phyllis Hamilton bred her. She doesn't quite have the look of Phyllis's dogs. Phyllis's dogs have small ears, not that these are all that big, and Phyllis's dogs have plenty of facial markings, more than this. Do you know anything about her?"

"Nope."

"And my utility bills? My bank statement? These are recent. I'm not sure when I threw this stuff out. Just before Labor Day? Kevin, I don't like that."

"That was what made 'em think she was you."

"Who is she? You must know by now. What's all the secrecy about?"

"We don't know much yet, but, yeah, she's unidentified. There was a purse there, but it'd been emptied. No cash, no ID in it, junk dumped out. Lipsticks, empty wallet. The neighbors say that this Dr. Ho had a house sitter lined up, and the guy backed out at the last minute. He didn't want to leave it empty because of the plants and the fish."

"Fish," I said. "I can never quite get that. They're pretty. But why keep pets that don't love you back? Anyway, speaking of fish, I heard that Dr. Ho picks up women at Loaves and Fishes. The neighbors think that's what happened."

Kevin shrugged. "No luck reaching him."

"He's in Africa. That's what I heard. What else was in the house? What else that belonged to the woman, I mean."

"Stuff in the name of Holly Winter." Kevin is not normally laconic. He was working away at the steak and trying not to talk with his mouth full.

"Kevin, you just showed me that. What else?"

84

"The other one, too."

I helped myself to a french fry. "The other Holly Winter? There were things of hers there, too?"

Kevin nodded.

"Bills and stuff from her trash? Kevin, look, this whole situation is weird for me. Could you please give the steak a rest and talk to me?"

He put down his knife and fork, wiped his mouth, and looked me in the eye. "It looks like someone got into the other one's apartment. She was in England for the summer. Lah-di-dah. She just got back on Tuesday. And she left a key hidden where nobody'd ever guess. You got it: under the doormat. You see, the way it works is that the world's divided in two, the smart and stupid, and the way you tell the smart ones, they're at Harvard, and it's a whole other world there, so —"

"She went to England for the summer and left her key under the doormat? What did she expect? Harvard. I thought she had some connection with Harvard."

"ABD. Does that mean something to you?"

"All but dissertation. In what?"

"Statistics. She works, too. Teaches a course. Consults, whatever that means. And she knows this Dr. Ho. They're not friends. She says they know each other from some group that hates Superman. What's wrong with Superman?"

"It's not just Superman, Kevin. It's media characters in general."

"I gotta tell you, Holly, you're being a lot nicer about this than she is. Wants to know everything, wants to see everything, wants action. She's wicked pissed."

"At a woman who had the misfortune to be murdered? Well, I don't exactly like it that the woman went through my trash, but she obviously got a lot worse than she deserved. Kevin, is all this about identity theft? Because I don't think my identity's been stolen. I do all my banking online. I keep a close eye on everything, and there hasn't been anything suspicious."

"Checked your credit lately?"

"No. But I will. Kevin, did she say anything about the guy on the motorcycle? The one I told you about. Adam. Did he show up at her house?"

" 'Preposterous notion.' That's a quote."

"He said something about someone named Calvin. Had I heard from Calvin? Or maybe had Calvin said something . . . I don't remember. Yes I do. He said, 'You haven't heard from Calvin?' As if I should have. Or as if he expected me to have heard from Calvin, whoever he is. I was so angry at Leah for leaving this guy, Adam, in the house that I wasn't paying all that much attention. Did I tell you about that? Leah let him in, and when she went out, she left him sitting in my kitchen. I mean, Leah reads Latin, she's taken all these premed courses for vet school, she gets As, and she can be totally brainless. It sometimes seems to me that Harvard ought to have a required course on common sense."

"I hope you chewed her out."

"I did. She won't do it again. Or she won't do exactly the same thing again. But I worry about her."

"Speaking of that, there's one other thing."

"Kevin, I know what's coming. The cop-mentality lecture, right? The world is a dangerous place. We all have to stay on high alert all the time, or we'll —"

"She was younger than you. Early twenties or so. Different, uh, style. Long fingernails, nail polish, lots of makeup. Capri pants. Is that what you call them? And those high-heeled sandals with no backs. She smoked. Traces of methamphetamine. Whole other world from you."

"Good," I said.

He dug back into his steak. I passed the

time by nibbling on a few french fries. Finally, I said, "And?"

"There's this other thing."

"What? What other thing?"

"I'm not saying she was some kind of twin of yours or anything."

"Her hair. Kevin, you seem to have forgotten that I saw her. Not her face, but I did notice her hair. It was about the same color as mine. Same length."

"Same height as you, more or less. Same build."

"Average height, ordinary build."

"She dyed her hair."

"This is my natural color."

"Like I said, she dyed her hair the color of yours."

"And the color of a million other people's! For all we know, it's the most popular shade of hair coloring in America. Well, it probably isn't. It's too reddish for most people. But if you're suggesting that she was trying to look like me, that's . . . let me quote the other Holly Winter. It's a preposterous notion."

"And the picture of the dog?"

"The photo you brought with you has to be a copy. Of course it is. You must have other copies. I want this one. I've never seen this malamute before, but I'm going to a show tomorrow, and I can hand it around. There'll be other malamute people there. There's one person in particular who knows everything about blue malamutes. Phyllis Hamilton. I mentioned her before. She has a dog entered. I want to show this picture to her."

"Go ahead."

We ate silently for a minute. Then I said, "Kevin? Not that I buy this theory of yours. Not at all. But . . . you said she wasn't some kind of twin of mine. But was there . . . ?"

"Like I said."

"Hair, height, build. Her face?"

"Not really."

"What about this other Holly Winter?"

"What about her?"

"Kevin, talk to me! Do you think that the dead woman was trying to look like her, too?"

"Nope. The other one's a scrawny little thing with a short haircut. Severe-looking woman, dark brown hair, all bones. Five feet, five-one. No resemblance, not to you, not to the victim."

"Not that I care," I said. "Really, this Holly Winter and I have nothing in common except the planned identity theft. Or thefts. Plural. And that must just have been a matter of convenience. If you're going to steal identities, it's probably easier and simpler to use one name instead of two, isn't it? Especially since we both live in Cambridge. And that's all there was to it." I paused. "Unless . . . Kevin, does the other Holly Winter happen to own a dog?"

"Hates them," he said. "Hates the sight of them."

I felt oddly pleased. "Well, that settles it," I said. "From a cosmic perspective, we have nothing in common at all."

CHAPTER 10

My father, Buck, is in his element at a dog show. That's because his element is a place where he can cause maximum embarrassment with a minimum of effort. My stepmother, Gabrielle, disagrees. They met at a show when Gabrielle was new to the dog game, and in what I'm sure was his most mooselike fashion, Buck stomped in and, according to Gabrielle, poured oil on troubled waters. Nonsense! What does a moose know about oil? I am convinced that Buck trampled down underbrush, tore up saplings, felled trees, locked horns, and bellowed. He always does. But Gabrielle was smitten. According to her, Buck made everything fun.

At the moment, he, at least, was having fun, or so I assumed from the irritating smile plastered on his big face. "What'd you want to go and hire a handler for?" he was demanding in that deep, booming voice of his. "You were the best little junior handler in New England. Why, I remember the time —"

"A time that I am sure no one wants to hear about," I said quietly. "Or in my case, remember."

It was nine thirty on a clear, bright Saturday morning. Rowdy, Sammy, and I had had as smooth a trip from Cambridge as Steve's rattletrap van allowed. The site of the Yankee Spirit Kennel Club show was a fairgrounds in northern Connecticut. I am crazy about outdoor shows, but only if the weather cooperates. Drenching rain ruins even the best grooming job, and mud spoils all the work I do on the dogs' beautiful white legs and feet. Worse, Rowdy reliably expresses his objection to water, and to summer heat as well, by moping, balking, and otherwise presenting himself to the judge as a droopy sourpuss. Today was Rowdy's kind of day, dry and cool, and the show was my kind of show, an outdoor festivity with those big white tents that suggest a wedding at a Camelot gone nuts over purebred dogs. We were now under one of the tents in an area packed with grooming tables, crates, folding chairs, tack boxes, powerful dryers, and extension cords, not to mention dogs, owners, and handlers. My father and Gabrielle, who'd driven down from Maine the day before and had spent the night in a motel, had done me the favor of transporting and setting up a grooming table, a dryer, and two big Vari Kennels now occupied by Rowdy and Sammy.

"Your father is just joking," said Gabrielle, who always makes that excuse for Buck. Reality to the contrary, she may even believe it. As far as I can tell, she is blindly in love with him. As for Buck, what baffles me is the good sense he showed in falling hard for a warm, considerate, flexible, and altogether delightful woman. It's possible that Gabrielle's good looks fooled him into imagining that she was as impossible as he is. Although she's somewhat plump and has fair skin that shows sun damage, her refusal to diet and to use sunscreen almost highlights the loveliness of her bone structure. When I first met her, I thought that her hair was making a natural transition from blond to gray. I now know that the gray is more natural than the blond, but I had to be told; and if I didn't know better, I'd also assume that she chose her clothing at random and luckily ended up in soft, loose outfits that just so happened to suit her. As to Gabrielle's ownership of the fluffy little all-white Molly, let me quote the American Kennel

Club standard for the bichon frise: "Gentle mannered, sensitive, playful, and affectionate. A cheerful attitude is the hallmark of the breed."

"What Buck tells me," Gabrielle continued, "is that if you want something done right, you should hire a professional. And I do. I always use a handler for Molly."

" 'To every thing there is a season,' " pronounced my father, " 'and a time to every purpose under heaven.' "

What he meant by *under heaven* was, I should explain, *on the grounds of a dog show.*

"Okay," I conceded, "some breeds are harder to owner-handle than others, at least if you want to win."

"If winning's all you care about," said Buck, "why'd you go and fire Faith?"

Oh, he is infuriating! First of all, showing dogs is incredibly competitive, as he of all people knew; second, he himself was competition personified; and third, no matter how well Faith had handled Rowdy and no matter how often he'd won with her, Buck had done nothing but criticize every single thing about her. And now this!

"We have had a parting of the ways," I said. Faith had failed to turn up one time too many, and she'd violated our agreement that if she weren't available, she'd provide a substitute professional handler. "I've watched Teller handle a million times, and so have you. You know how good he is."

John Teller, who was always called by his last name, was first-rate. Like a lot of other top professional handlers, he moved with a dancer's grace and had an uncanny ability to connect with dogs and bring out the best in them. Also, judges knew exactly who he was, and that knowledge never hurts.

"Politics," Buck spat out. "It's an insult to Rowdy. He doesn't need that SOB. And what about Sammy?"

"Teller is providing a handler for Sammy in case we need one."

This is a bit of oversimplification, but here goes: Sammy, who hadn't finished his championship, was entered in the regular class called Open Dogs. Teller was going to handle him there. If Sammy won that class and then beat the winners of the other regular classes (Puppy, Novice, Bred by Exhibitor, and American Bred) to go Winners Dog, then he, together with the Winners Bitch, the top female competing for championship points, would end up in the Best of Breed competition. Rowdy, however, was what's called a "special," a champion eligible only for the Best of Breed competition, where he'd go up against the Winners

Dog, the Winners Bitch, and the other specials. Consequently, if Sammy went WD, both of my dogs would be in the ring at the same time, and we'd need two handlers, Teller for Rowdy, a second handler for Sammy.

"So, is this your first show?" Buck demanded. "You're so new to this that you trust this guy?"

"Phyllis!" I exclaimed a little too loudly. "Over here!"

I was always glad to see Phyllis Hamilton, who was, as I'd told Kevin, an expert on blue malamutes, in fact, *the* person best qualified to comment on the photo found at the murder scene. She was also a friend of mine and just the sort of sympathetic, considerate person who'd be happy to distract my father and thus get him to let up on me. Phyllis showed her dogs all the time. Consequently, she knew Buck and thus knew exactly what he was like. The only unfortunate thing about Phyllis's arrival was that she wore show-ring attire, a neat pantsuit with a plaid jacket, and was obviously going to handle the malamute she had with her, a lovely seal-and-white bitch who looked about Sammy's age.

Before Phyllis had even reached us, my father started up again. "Now, you see?

There's no reason on God's green earth why you can't do what Phyllis does. She handles her youngsters herself, and she uses a handler for —"

"Phyllis, your bitch is beautiful! What's her name?" I asked.

"Heart. This is Benchmark Heart's Desire," said Phyllis in that distinctive voice of hers, well-bred and musical.

The canine introduction having been performed, I greeted Phyllis properly and introduced her to Gabrielle. "And you know my father," I added, without appending any obvious phrase such as *unfortunately for you* or *to my everlasting embarrassment*.

Gabrielle responded graciously, and Buck, as I'd hoped, shifted his attention to Heart, who reciprocated by wagging her beautiful plumy white tail and bestowing on him the sort of adoring gaze that he inevitably elicits from dogs. I was itching to get Phyllis's opinion of the blue malamute in the photo, but I had no intention of telling my father anything about the murder and, in particular, anything about the apparent intent to steal my identity and the finding of the photo among the victim's possessions. Buck viewed Cambridge and all other cities outside the state of Maine as dangerous. Buck was right in the sense that Maine does have a low murder rate, principally because everyone knows that everyone else has a gun, or so my father always argued. With the intention of transforming Cambridge into Augusta, Portland, or Bangor, Buck had once given me a Smith & Wesson Lady-Smith, as I intended to remind him if he heard about the murder and threatened to move in with me to serve as my bodyguard until Steve returned. DoG forbid! If you want to know what Buck is like as a house-guest, consider that the revolver was, incredibly, a hostess gift, my father's notion of an appropriate alternative to a good bottle of wine or a florist-delivered basket of fresh flowers.

Checking my watch, I saw that we had an hour until malamutes were due in the ring. I'd already had Rowdy and Sammy on the grooming table, so they'd need only a few spritzes of water and a bit of fluffing up with a brush to be ready. Phyllis wouldn't need more than a few minutes to study the photo and talk to me about it, and I wanted to catch her now, before the malamute judging, in case she had plans for later. I retrieved the photo from my gear bag, where it had been protected by a plastic bag and sheets of cardboard.

Phyllis and Gabrielle were intent on

another glossy print, a show photo of Gabrielle's bichon, Molly. Surrounded by the elements of the show scene, their gazes fixed on the picture of the bichon, their heads bent at the same angle, they made such an appealing picture that I wished that I had a camera handy. Their hair, I noticed, was almost the same shade of blond. Phyllis's was a bit shorter than Gabrielle's, but the similarity of coloring and their identical poses made them look like sisters. I wished I could capture the image and hated to interrupt.

Fortunately, I didn't need to. Spotting the print in my hand, Gabrielle said, "You finally have new pictures for me!"

"I do at home," I said. "But this is one I want Phyllis's opinion about. It's a blue malamute."

Why in Buck's presence was I stupid enough to say that I wanted someone else's opinion of a dog? Won't I ever learn? Before Phyllis had a chance to take the photo from my hand, Buck seized it and, worse, held it so that no one else could see it at all.

"Blue," he said. "You got that right."

"Is your name Phyllis Hamilton?" I demanded.

"Of course that's her name," said Buck, whose misunderstanding was, I felt certain, deliberate and controlling. "You've known Phyllis for years. Holly, are you all right?"

"Buck," said Gabrielle, "others would like to look, too."

"Dilute seal," said my father. "A bitch."

If I'd had a second copy of the photo with me, I'd have risked tearing this one by snatching it back. As it was, I left matters to Gabrielle, who reached up, plucked the picture from Buck's hand, gave it to Phyllis, and said to my father, "What an odd color! Blue? Is that what you call it?"

A professional handler hired to manage Buck couldn't have done better. My father took Gabrielle's bait and began to lecture her about coat color in the Alaskan malamute and the genetics of coat color in dogs. As he went on about sable, mahogany sable, red, black, and Alaskan seal, not to mention gray, wolf gray, dark wolf gray, all white, and tricolor, for example, and then about pigmentation, alleles, homozygosity, modifiers, and the recessive d, I said softly to Phyllis, "What can you tell me about her?" I did not, I might mention, apologize for Buck's behavior, nor did I sigh, roll my eyes, or say that although the notion that a wife should have to manage her husband was abhorrent to me, I still felt unbounded gratitude to my stepmother for doing just that.

"How old is she?" asked Phyllis, meaning, of course, the blue malamute and not Gabrielle.

"I have no idea. I'm guessing four or five. Not old, I guess. But what do you think?"

Phyllis nodded. "Mature. Not a puppy."

"I really don't know a thing about her. All I have is this picture." I lowered my voice to the softest whisper. "A cop gave it to me. I don't want to talk about that in front of Buck." At normal volume, I said, "I don't think she's from your lines. Her ears look a little big. Not gigantic, but bigger than in your dogs. And I'd expect more facial markings. But I could be wrong."

"No, you're right," Phyllis said. "And she is a dilute seal and white, but she's not from my lines."

To avoid sounding like my father, let me limit myself to saying that a seal-and-white malamute is what most people would and, in fact, often do call black and white. A true black and white, however, has a dark undercoat beneath the black outercoat — the coarse, water-repellant guard coat — whereas a seal and white has a light undercoat. At the risk of sounding exactly like Buck, I also need to say that the recessive d gene dilutes black to what is called "blue."

"Have you ever seen her?"

"No. I'd remember."

"I know you would. Do you have any idea where she could've come from?" My question was about bloodlines. An established kennel with a careful breeding program develops a characteristic style of dog, and someone with a deep knowledge of a breed can sometimes spot a family resemblance. Sometimes. Not always.

"It's hard to say. Let me think about it. Something . . . there's something I can't put my finger on."

Once again, I resorted to whispering. "I'll call you and tell you the whole story."

"Sorry not to be able to help more. I'll have to think about it. I'll be home on Monday."

"Keep the picture." I'd scanned the one Kevin had given me. "And we'll talk when you're home."

Phyllis smiled warmly. "Holly, your father?" She paused. "Buck is such a . . . presence." She paused again. "Get his opinion, too. Don't discount what he has to say. He has a good eye for a dog."

Phyllis was right. Furthermore, as was about to be demonstrated, he had an infuriating habit of making himself obnoxious about something and then — damn it all — turning out to be right.

CHAPTER 11

Twenty minutes later, when my handlers showed up, Phyllis and Heart had left, Rowdy was still crated, and I had Sammy back on the grooming table. The tented grooming area had aisles of sorts formed by rows of crates and other paraphernalia. Buck and Gabrielle were in the next aisle, about fifteen feet away, where they were talking to a personage in the dog fancy named Lewis Van Zandt, whom I'd known since my childhood, when he used to greet me by pinching me hard on the cheek. My mother had forbidden me to retaliate, but she'd had no influence on Buck, who had waited for the next episode to teach the personage a lesson. My moose of a father must've been a foot taller than the diminutive Van Zandt, and instead of quickly pinching and releasing the little man's cheek, Buck got a good grip on a fold of flesh and shook hard in the manner of a big dog pretending to break the neck of a stuffed toy. I couldn't have been more than seven years old, but the image of Buck's revenge remains vivid and powerful. To this day, I am grateful. To this day, too, Buck prods and baits Van Zandt, who is terrified of Buck, or so I assume. Why else would Van Zandt still speak to him?

But as I was saying, Rowdy's handler, Teller, appeared, and trailing after him was the second handler he'd promised to supply. Teller was a round-faced, muscular man of medium height, heavy around the middle, but light on his feet, and he was groomed and dressed in a fashion intended to convey respect for the judges. He had short brown hair and was so closely shaved that I wondered whether he might have used a depilatory on his face. He wore gray pants with sharp creases, a tweed sport coat, a white shirt, and a red tie. Although he'd probably been showing dogs since the early morning, he looked fresh and energetic, and not a single hair, dog or human, was evident on his attire. In brief, Teller looked worth the fee I was paying him.

"Hey, Holly," he greeted me. "Rowdy's looking good."

"This is Sammy," I said. "Rowdy's in his crate."

"Dead ringer," Teller said. "This is Omar."

"Nice to meet you," I said.

The name was misleading. Omar had pale blond hair and fair, badly sunburned skin. His hazel eyes looked faded and weak, as if they had once belonged to a nonagenarian and had been transplanted to his sockets by mistake. The remainder of Omar's face, including his vapid expression, suggested a maximum age of twenty.

After fruitlessly waiting for Omar to say that it was nice to meet me, too, I said bluntly, "Are you sure you're up for this? You've handled malamutes before, haven't you?"

Omar's sport coat and the rest of his attire were appropriate for the ring, but his manner was, at best, unimpressive, and his build was disconcertingly frail. He looked too slight to handle a frisky Chihuahua.

"He's trained, isn't he?" Omar said.

"Yes," I began, "but —"

Teller cut me off. "Omar's a pro."

The sound of my father's characteristic bellow distracted me. Glancing toward him, I saw that he and Gabrielle were still talking to Lewis Van Zandt. Actually, Gabrielle and Van Zandt were silent; Buck was doing all the talking, and he was doing it loudly enough so that everyone within a mile must've heard every single word he was saying. I listened in horror.

"Growing marijuana!" Buck exclaimed. "My wife! Who'd ever have thought? It was all in the *Ellsworth American.* We had a visit from the DEA. That's the Drug Enforcement Administration. Pleasant young fellow. You'd never guess to look at Gabrielle, would you? Looks as —"

"Teller," I said hastily, "you'll have to pick up the armbands. Rowdy's in this crate." I pointed. "I'll see you . . . I'll see you later."

Lewis Van Zandt had no sense of humor. What's more, he was none too bright. To make matters worse, he was a dreadful rumormonger. And Buck was baiting him with some ludicrous tale about Gabrielle, marijuana, and the DEA? While simultaneously spreading the story himself at top volume? Buck knew exactly how gossipy shows were; and gossip being the distorting phenomenon that it is, word would be out that Buck and Gabrielle had been freebasing cocaine or dealing heroin at this very show.

Without actually leaping over crates, I managed to reach Van Zandt, Buck, and the maligned Gabrielle in what must have been seconds. "He's only joking," I assured the old cheek-pincher. "You know Buck. He can never resist the temptation to —"

To my horror, Gabrielle said, "No, no, it's perfectly true! Not that I've been growing marijuana, of course, but we did have a visit from a DEA agent. It was all very exciting! He belongs to a special *team.* We thought he sounded very proud of it, just as if he played for the Red Sox. He told us all about *drugs.* It seems that this kind of marijuana patch is much more common in *southern* Maine than it is in our part of the state, although I have to wonder whether it isn't just a matter of where people get *caught.* It could be the climate, too, I suppose. But these DEA *teams* aren't all that interested in marijuana, anyway. The one they're worried about is . . . Buck, what's it called?"

"Methamphetamine."

"That's it! He was telling us that as it is, there's not a lot of it in Maine. Holly, do you know that these terrible people mail it to Maine from Arizona and places like that? They mail it! Or they use UPS or FedEx. Just like L.L.Bean! But in reverse! So, the purpose of this team is to make them stop. And to stop them from making it. It's quite easy to, uh, brew, I suppose you'd say. All you —"

"There was obviously some mistake," I said to Lewis Van Zandt. "Gabrielle is the last person who'd do anything illegal.

Maybe it was someone with the same name."

"No, they had the right person," Gabrielle insisted. "And it was my land."

"A wood lot in Washington County," Buck said.

"In the Unorganized Territories," Gabrielle added. "Isn't that a wonderful expression? It makes Maine sound like the wild frontier!"

To Van Zandt, I said, "It means that the state of Maine collects the real estate taxes for areas without organized townships. What must've happened was that Gabrielle owned some land that someone else used to —"

"I'm far from sure that I like this image of myself as a Goody Two-shoes," Gabrielle said.

As I was struggling to find a way to impress precisely that image of her on Lewis Van Zandt without simultaneously offending Gabrielle, my father said, "We're going to miss the judging if we don't get going."

Damn it all! He was right. If I'd missed the judging entirely, it would've been his fault. Van Zandt didn't accompany us to the ring, either because he didn't want to be seen with a family of notorious drug dealers or because he could hardly wait to spread the word of our notoriety. I was relieved to be rid of him and also happy to have a few moments to remind Buck of the dog-show maxim that says, keep your eyes and ears open and your mouth shut.

Unchastened, Buck said, "Well, the old fool didn't pinch your cheek today, did he?"

As we made our way to the ring where malamutes were about to be judged, Buck expanded on one of his favorite themes, namely, the obligation of every one of us to experience and express overwhelming joy and gratitude in response to the multifarious beauties of nature that surrounded us. The beauties of nature he had in mind were the golden retrievers, Alaskan malamutes, Akitas, West Highland white terriers, German shepherd dogs, Belgian sheepdogs, and so forth and so on that did, in fact, surround us and were, in fact, wonderfully diverse and extraordinarily beautiful and thus cause for joy and gratitude.

" 'The world is so full of a number of things, I'm sure we should all be as happy as kings,' " Buck proclaimed.

We had missed only the beginning of the malamute judging. As we approached the ring, my father consulted the show catalog and said, "She's going to do Open now. Small entry. Pitiful. I don't know why you bothered."

"Because *you* told me to." Almost whispering, I said, "You told me that a friend of a friend of yours said that Mrs. Woofenden was going to draw a very small entry and asked you as a big favor to see if you could help. I bothered because you leaned on me and because I am a good sport and a nice person. As you perfectly well know, all Sammy needs is one major, and this isn't a major. He's here because *you* wanted him entered." Let's settle for saying that all Sammy needed to finish his championship was one more big win, a "major," and that today's entry was too small to count. In normal tones, I added, "And Rowdy? Buck, is this your first show? I'm interested in the Group."

Summary: breeds are judged first. The Best of Breed winners, one for each breed, then compete in the judging of the Groups to which they belong. If Rowdy went BOB, Best of Breed, as I hoped he'd do, he'd then compete in the Working Group, which is to say, the judging of the BOB winners from the breeds that belonged to the Working Group: the Akita, the Siberian husky, the Rottweiler, the Newfoundland, and so on. Apples and oranges? Not really. Anyway, Rowdy had a good chance of going BOB, and I wanted a placement in the group.

Placement: first through fourth place, preferably guess which one, but it's an honor to place in the group at all. Incidentally, my hope for a group placement was why I'd entered two dogs who might compete against each other for Best of Breed and why Teller would handle Rowdy in Best of Breed: if Rowdy went BOB, thus getting his ticket to the group, I thought he'd place there, whereas Sammy, gorgeous though he was, just didn't have the maturity to be serious competition in the group.

Anyway, when I'd finished telling Buck what he already knew, I spotted my dogs and my handlers, and I went flying to the ring, where Mrs. Woofenden was about to judge Open Dogs, that is, Sammy's class, which consisted of males that had not completed their championships. Into that ring, my expensive professional handler, Teller, was leading my special, my champion, my consistent group placer, namely Rowdy. Mindful of the AKC's prohibition against creating any sort of disturbance at a show, I came to a halt next to Teller and Rowdy and said in the softest voice I could manage, "Teller, stop! You have the wrong dog!"

CHAPTER 12

I am happy to report that the mix-up had no serious consequences. Indeed, if I hadn't appeared in time to prevent Teller from showing Rowdy in place of Sammy, the result wouldn't have been disastrous; everyone, including Mrs. Woofenden, would've understood that Teller had made an innocent mistake, albeit a stupid and careless one. Rowdy and Sammy, father and son, did look a lot alike, especially to people who didn't know them. Still, it's almost certain that one of the other exhibitors or spectators would've spotted the error; Rowdy was so well known that someone would've recognized him and spoken up. Teller had no excuse; even if he'd never seen Rowdy before, he should've known which dog was which. Sammy lacked Rowdy's physical maturity; he hadn't quite finished filling out. Furthermore, Rowdy's superb natural showmanship and his experience in the ring meant that he shifted into show-off mode well outside the baby gates, whereas Sammy's demeanor was puppyish. As to the actual show results, Sammy went Winners Dog, Phyllis's Heart went Winners Bitch and Best of Winners, and Rowdy took the breed and got a Group II, so I couldn't complain, especially because the Newf that won the Group was really something. Gabrielle's bichon, Molly, won her breed but went nowhere in the Group. Gabrielle, however, wasn't yet a hardcore show type, which is to say that she honestly did not mind losing. Give her a few more years with my father, and that attitude would change.

When Buck, Gabrielle, the three dogs, and I finally reached Cambridge, I got my guests settled in their room, and we sat at the kitchen table and ate beef stew. My father was in a good mood and on good behavior. Why not? He'd embarrassed me at a show, and he'd been more or less right about Teller. Also, since I'd managed to keep Buck ignorant of the murder and the Holly Winter mix-up, he had no excuse to turn protective. Following Phyllis's suggestion, I got him talking about blue malamutes. Buck knew that I was active in Alaskan Malamute Rescue of New England and in the national group, the Alaskan Malamute Assistance

League, and he knew that Phyllis Hamilton also did malamute rescue. Consequently, he made the natural mistake of assuming that the blue malamute in the photo was a rescue dog. I didn't correct him. Unfortunately, he had nothing useful to say. He knew the names of a few old-time malamute kennels, including Sena Lak, Blue Ice, and Sugarbear, that had produced blue, and he recommended an article I'd already read, a piece written by the late Jane Wilson-Adickes.

Although I'd warned Kevin about Buck's visit and implored him to say nothing to my father about the murder, I was still worried throughout the meal that Kevin might pop in and mention the dead woman and the possible identity theft, but the fear was needless. Over dessert, Gabrielle talked with delighted animation about the DEA's discovery that someone had been growing marijuana on her land. In itself, the incident amounted to nothing. The property was a forty-acre lot in a numbered township that didn't even have a name. The neighbors, if you can call them that, were big paper companies rather than people, and some unknown person had taken advantage of the isolation of Gabrielle's land to grow marijuana in what was evidently a small clearing. Gabrielle and her late husband had bought the lot twenty years earlier. She paid taxes on it but had never so much as seen it. When I extracted details about the drug agent's visit, I realized that it had been pro forma; the agent had informed Gabrielle about the situation, and that had been that. I am proud to report that instead of taking Buck to task for having started a rumor that would be broadcast throughout the dog fancy, I kept my eyes and ears open and my mouth shut.

Buck, Gabrielle, and Molly left early on Sunday morning. It was a wet, dreary day, and I found myself missing Steve as well as wishing that Leah were still living with us and that Rita were home or returning at any minute. For once, there wasn't a single dog-related event nearby that I wanted to attend. There were friends I could've called but no one I wanted to see, and the prospect of going alone to a concert or a bookstore made me feel like Eleanor Rigby. Work? On a Sunday? I'm my own employer and a good one: I give myself weekends off. I do household chores, of course, as I did that morning. I changed the sheets in the bedroom, vacuumed, and performed the routine task required to keep Sammy's beloved Pink Piggy working. The toy that Steve and I called Pink Piggy was a Dr. Noy's toy, a purple pig, a plush toy that had a great feature: the squeaker was replaceable. For reasons that baffled me, Sammy had never torn Pink Piggy to shreds, but he killed the squeakers all the time. I always kept a supply of fresh ones on hand. It took almost no time to rip open the Velcro on Pink Piggy's back, remove the pouch inside, pull out the dead squeaker, slip in the new one, insert the pouch, and close the toy up. Then I had to repeat the process because, in the manner of Betty Burley and Kimi, Pink Piggy manifested itself in three simultaneous incarnations that were indistinguishable from one another and thus all went by the same name.

When I'd finished restoring Pink Piggy's voice, I spent some time training Rowdy and then Sammy. After that, I checked my e-mail, printed out a fresh copy of the photo of the blue malamute, ran off more copies of the lost-dog flyer, and then, on inspiration, searched through the Alaskan Malamute Registry Pedigree Program, a database with information about more than 79,000 malamutes from all over the world. The database includes all the malamutes in the American Kennel Club Stud Book Register, in studbooks from other countries, and in other published sources. The simplest use of the program is to generate the family trees beloved by fanciers of purebred dogs, but it can also be used to search for malamutes that meet particular criteria, for example, dogs with the sire or dam you enter; dogs with a specified kennel name, breeder, or owner; dogs with a given birth date; and so forth. A little poking around in the database, however, soon demonstrated what the program's creator, Dan Anderson, had once told me, namely, that searching by color had more than a few hitches. Among other things, malamutes come in a bewildering variety of colors; knowledgeable people use a great variety of terms for the myriad of colors; and worse yet, official systems, which radically over-simplify coat color, have changed over the years. For instance, malamute fanciers may disagree about whether a particular all-white dog's shading is biscuit, cream, or off-white; and once-popular terms like *wolf gray* and *wolf sable* have fallen out of use because neither the American Kennel Club nor malamute fanciers are eager to encourage the general public to confuse purebred Alaskan malamutes with wolves or wolf dogs. Well, I'll skip to the result, which was that my search yielded only a handful of malamutes coded as blue. Next, I searched for dogs with the word *blue* in their registered names. That search identified 563 dogs, including some that clearly were — or had been — the real thing and not simply dogs named for blues songs. For instance, the color code "ChclBlWh" obviously meant the charcoal-black shade of blue, and some of the dogs bore the names of kennels known to produce — or to have produced — blue, including Phyllis's Benchmark, as well as Sena Lak, Warlock, Blue Ice, Sugarbear, Snosquall, Ice Age, Crevasse, and Blueline.

Whoops! Maybe I need to explain the names of registered purebred dogs. Take Sammy. His registered name is Jazzland's As Time Goes By. *Jazzland* is the kennel name of his breeder, Cindy Neely. In daily life, of course, Steve and I make fools of ourselves over dogs all the time, but not to the extent of calling our dog by saying, "Come, Jazzland's As Time Goes By!" Really, there are limits. So, Sammy's call name is Sammy.

At the end of about an hour with the database, when I started to search for dogs with potentially bluish names like Cornflower, Denim, Ultramarine, Sapphire, and Wedgwood, I could feel my thoughts turning various shades of Alice, baby, electric, robin's egg, or possibly neon blue, so I quit for the day and ran to the little store on Concord Avenue for milk. Rain was still falling, and the sky was a deep slate, gunmetal, steel, or . . .

Anyway, as I was coming out of the shop, I ran into Mellie, who was swathed in a gigantic red plastic poncho that made her look like a Mylar balloon. When we'd exchanged greetings, I asked what she was doing here. As I suspected, she'd been to Mass at Saint Peter's. Neither of us had any news about Strike. I was carrying some lost-dog flyers that I'd intended to put around my neighborhood, but I gave them to Mellie instead. I said that I'd been sending e-mail. Did Mellie understand what I meant? Mellie said she'd been lighting candles and praying to the Virgin. Did I truly understand what she meant? In any case, so far, neither of us had a reply.

CHAPTER 13

On that same Sunday morning, the other Holly Winter also searches databases. Those of interest to her, however, contain information on human beings and specifically on human beings named Holly Winter. The Argali directory lists eleven of us, two in Cambridge, of course, and the remaining nine dispersed throughout the United States in the manner of chain-store franchises, an image, I should note, that occurs to me, the dog-loving Holly Winter, and not to the unfanciful Holly Winter who thinks of images as graphics that display data. By searching other directories, she discovers 154 listings for us, but to her annoyance, there are many obvious duplications. Even so, she prints the complete listing of our addresses and phone numbers.

As to her interest in me, she finds that the database for the City of Cambridge shows the property at 256 Concord Avenue as having a land area of 4,004 square feet; and the building, a living area of 2,819 square feet. The Exterior Wall Type is coded as WOOD-SHN-SHK, the Roof Material as ASPHALT-SHNG. Those dopes at city hall! Why not pick one abbreviation for *shingle* and stick to it? The assessed value, which is, I am happily convinced, below the market value, strikes her as high. The photograph shows a simple three-story red house with white trim and a little porch. What I find to be the charm of the place is lost on her.

Google provides a tremendous amount of information about me. In particular, the other Holly discovers the opportunity to learn far more than she wants to know about dogs. That's not hard: what she wants to know about dogs is absolutely nothing.

CHAPTER 14

When I say that I never work on weekends, I mean that I don't sit down and write. Because my work and play are both about dogs, my weekend play often does end up as the subject of a column or an article. For instance, when I returned home after my brief encounter with Mellie, I worked on a little project destined to find its way into print, namely the construction and application of what's known as Shirley Chong's doggie nail file. Unfortunately, I don't know Shirley Chong, who is a dog trainer and, as her invention proves, an outright genius. Here's the problem she solved: A lot of dogs hate having their nails cut, and a lot of dog owners hate doing canine manicures. The usual method requires the owner to grasp the dog's paw and use clippers to trim the nails without hitting the quick. If the dog squirms, it's easy to take off so much nail that the dog yelps in pain, bleeds all over everything, and forever after turns tail at the sight of clippers. What's more, even experienced owners who can see and avoid the veins in light nails find it difficult not to quick black nails. At best, traditional nail trimming is a necessary but joyless process. With Shirley Chong's nail file, the dog not only files his own nails but has a grand time doing it. Or that was the idea.

I'd printed out the instructions from the Web site, www.shirleychong.com/keepers/nailfile.html, and on a recent trip to the hardware store had bought the kind of adhesive tape that's applied to steps to prevent people from slipping. My basement had supplied a spare board about a foot across and three feet long. It took almost no time to stick the tape to the board and thus to construct a malamute-sized, very coarse file. After that, I crated Rowdy and Sammy, supplied myself with a clicker and cubes of chicken and cheese, and set out to teach Kimi to rake her front paws on the giant emery board. I could've used food alone, but the clicker, a little noisemaker that you pair with treats, was meant to speed things up, and so it did. Ten minutes after we started, I was sitting on a kitchen chair with the board propped up in front of me and pinned in place by my feet and knees, and

Kimi was happily scraping the coarse surface with one front paw and then another. When she dragged her nails on the file, I clicked and fed her a treat. Magic! No, operant conditioning: behavior followed by positive reinforcement increases in frequency, intensity, and duration. Behavior: raking nails on board. Positive reinforcement: the clicker, a secondary reinforcer or event marker; and food, a primary reinforcer. Of course, I'd still have to trim Kimi's dewclaws the old way, and teaching her to do the nails on her hind feet would be a challenge. Even so, success!

As I was saying just that to Kimi, the doorbell rang, and she abandoned her new pursuit to dash to the front hall in the hope that UPS or FedEx was delivering goodies for dogs.

"Sunday," I said. "How do I explain that one? Nothing in this for you, good girl."

She was a good girl, too. Containing her impulse to leap on the door and subsequently to offer our unknown caller an exuberant and possibly unwelcome greeting, Kimi sat a yard away from the door. Her dark eyes were bright and eager, and her tail was brushing back and forth across the floor, but her stay was solid. I opened the door.

The woman was about my age. There ended the similarity. Her hair was dark and almost as short as a man's. She was only about five feet tall and so thin that everything about her was sharp and angular. Her nose was little and pointed, her eyes were dark and small, her lips were thin and pursed, and she had a slightly undershot bite. Her black jersey skirt and top could have been chosen to attract dog hair. On her bony little feet were black flats. She toed out badly. Although she wasn't carrying the usual clipboard, handouts, and petitions, I wondered whether she could be soliciting for some good cause. In a sense and from her viewpoint, I was right: the good cause was herself.

"Holly Winter," she said.

"Holly Winter," I said with a smile that she didn't return.

"May I come in?" Her tone was formal and cold.

"Of course. Kimi, okay. Good girl."

Holly Winter, the other, didn't even glance at Kimi, who, with the weird prescience that still unsettles me, headed directly for the living room. The woman's stiff manner had made me reluctant to return to the kitchen. She seemed anything but the kind of person who'd sit there chatting while my dog filed her own nails. On the contrary, the other Holly would, I sensed, consider the activity bizarre.

Our living room is perfectly conventional. It has a small fireplace, a couch, two upholstered chairs, and the usual lamps and low tables. My office is packed with trophies, ribbons, framed certificates, show photos, and other dog paraphernalia, but except in December when there's a Christmas tree loaded with dog ornaments in the living room, the decor is proof to myself that my life hasn't gone entirely to the dogs. The day was still so dark that I turned on three lights, but I just gestured my visitor to a chair and didn't offer coffee or tea. Kimi, too, withheld any welcoming overtures. Holly took a seat on one side of the fireplace, and I sat opposite her. Kimi lay down at my feet and watched my face.

"I'm sure you're aware of this horrible business," she said.

I nodded. "Of course."

"Zach Ho," she said.

"The owner of the house."

"A classmate of mine." In Cambridge, *classmate* means at Harvard, presumably on the grounds that other colleges have no class. "And an, uh, acquaintance. We serve on an advisory board together."

"As I understand it," I said, "he's in Africa and totally out of touch. Unless there's something I haven't heard? Have the police been able to reach him?"

"Oh, the police! The police are useless."

"That hasn't been my experience with the Cambridge police." By nature, I'm the sort of straightforward person who gets her hackles up and blurts out, *The hell they are, you condescending snot!* This my-experience tactic was Gabrielle's. It always worked for her. In fact, it more than worked: she ended up making friends with everyone. The DEA agent? He was probably calling her all the time for advice about dealing with his parents and improving his love life.

"Then your experience must be very limited," the other Holly said. "Or in a role other than mine."

"I don't know what you mean." That wasn't a Gabrielle tactic. I honestly missed the insinuation.

"As someone who is the victim of identity theft," she said, "I take a personal interest in finding out the facts."

My hackles were now up. "As opposed to an impersonal interest? My information was stolen, too, you know. The police must have told you that. The woman, the murdered woman, apparently went through my trash.

But she didn't actually commit identity theft. It certainly looks as if she intended to. But she hadn't done it, at least so far as I know. My bank accounts look fine. I'm going to check my credit. I just haven't gotten around to it yet. Have you?"

"Yes."

"And?"

She shrugged. "Nothing yet."

"The poor woman is dead. She's hardly in a position to steal anyone's identity. Yours, mine, or anyone else's. In comparison with what happened to her, our problems are nothing."

"I don't appreciate having my situation minimized and trivialized, and I have to ask myself why you have such an investment in downplaying a serious crime." A certain immobility of expression and stiffness of body gave her an androidlike quality.

"The serious crime is murder. Pilfering other people's bills and bank statements isn't in the same league."

"Were you in Cambridge this summer?"

"What does that have to do with anything?"

Kimi slowly rose to her feet and moved to the left side of my chair.

"I was abroad," said Holly Winter.

"I wasn't. So what?"

Holly Winter, too, stood up. As she headed for the door, she said, "Simple explanations are often best. If one were to set out to steal another's identity, how very, very easy to target a victim with one's *own* name."

"Leave," I said. "Leave now."

She did.

CHAPTER 15

I am no thief. And why would I steal some-one else's identity, anyway? The one I have suits me fine. I have no desire to purloin a substitute. As to the possibility of filching a second identity to add to the first, this one is as full and challenging as I can manage: Steve, of course, and Rowdy, Kimi, Sammy, India, Lady, Tracker the cat, my cousin Leah, friends I cherish, a career I love, a funky house in Cambridge, and my beloved stepmother. My father? Well, the possibility of trading Buck in has occasionally crossed my mind, but who knows what flaws the replacement might have? Buck is unstint-ingly generous with time, attention, love, and money, and he is crazy about dogs. What if the new model were a stingy dog hater? Among other things, having such a father would transform me, which is to say that it would ruin my life. As to keeping Buck and acquiring a second father, well,

Buck is quite enough, thank you. I'm unwilling to risk what could be insurmountable challenges. For example, what if I ended up with two of him?

But Holly Winter hadn't been imagining that I'd wanted to make off with her life as a whole; she'd been thinking exclusively of money. The thinly veiled accusation was outrageous. I am a person of good character. Furthermore, if someone else's Social Security number, bank account information, credit card numbers, and passwords fell into my possession, I'd immediately get in touch with their owner. If I wanted to use the information to commit financial fraud, I wouldn't even know how to begin.

Still, Holly Winter's suspicion that I had been involved in trying to steal her identity has perhaps left me permanently hypersensitive. Consequently, I want to emphasize that I did not steal a look at her e-mail. Rather, I acquired my knowledge of the message she sent to Dr. Zachary Ho in an honest fashion and did so only later, not on that same Sunday afternoon, when she sent it. But I do know the address she used and the content of the e-mail. The address was the one granted to Dr. Ho by his alma mater, that place down the street from my house that famously leaves its ineradicable mark on its graduates and, if they so choose, leaves its mark on their e-mail addresses, too, in the form of the extension @post.harvard.edu. As an aside, I will mention the obvious, namely, that I am a person who has devoted her life to dogs; who owns two male malamutes; and whose female malamute, Kimi, lifts her leg as a matter of routine and even tries to lift both hind legs simultaneously as a means of demonstrating her commitment to a peculiarly urinary version of women's rights extremism. In other words, when I say that Harvard leaves its mark, I'm not using some vague and possibly inaccurate figure of speech; I know what I'm talking about.

So, Holly Winter composes e-mail to Dr. Zachary Ho at ZachHo@post.harvard.edu. The post-dot-Harvard is simply a forwarding address, as the other Holly Winter knows: Harvard does not go so far as to provide Internet access to alumni; it just forwards mail. Even so, what Holly Winter seeks is the power to reach Zach Ho, in more senses than one, and power is what she trusts Harvard to have. After all, it's the second wealthiest nonprofit in the world, second to the Vatican, and if that's not power, what is?

Big dogs. My answer. Not hers.

This is not the first time she has ever e-mailed Zach Ho, but it is the first time she has ever sent an individual message to him. The members of the advisory board of the Cambridge Alliance for Media-free Preschools, CAMP, occasionally hold what I presume are media-free meetings at media-free households, but they also use e-mail to communicate with one another. Even when she sends a message to the group, she avoids the ubiquitous e-mail *Hi,* which offends her.

Dear Zach,
First, because I have been the victim of identity theft, let me state that I am the Holly Winter you know from Harvard and from CAMP. That having been stated, let me proceed.

As you may or may not have heard, a situation has arisen that involves both of us. The police insist that they have been trying to reach you about it, but since they are acting like morons, not to mention archetypes of paternalism, I think it best to get in touch with you directly.

In brief, your house sitter has been murdered. Her body was found in your house last Thursday by a woman named

Holly Winter (not me). The police are adamant that the victim is unidentified. Among her belongings, according to these ridiculous policemen, were financial records of mine suggestive of an effort to steal my identity. This other person with my name claims that various identifying items had been stolen from her trash, but I ask you! And she found the body!

I simply cannot believe that you left your house in the care of some stranger. Who was she? And do you know anything about this woman with my name who lives on Concord Avenue? I paid her a visit. She is not our type at all.

Finally, let me, as a fellow crime victim, express my empathy. I have not had my tangible possessions damaged, as you have, but the dead woman entered my flat during my absence, or so it seems, and it is, furthermore, galling to have had her help herself to a valued intangible of mine, namely, my name, as opposed to having had her death result in the destruction of readily replaceable tangibles, i.e., aquariums and fish. Now that I have returned from England, I have the advantage of being on the spot, whereas you are not. If there is anything

I can do for you, do let me know. Please get in touch!

Best,
Holly Winter

I was going to withhold my comments, but I ask you: "on the spot . . . you are not"! I was not and am not her *type,* but I do my best to edit out unintended rhymes. Furthermore, if I'm about to slip into Lauren Bacall mode by telling a man that if there's anything he wants, all he has to do is whistle, I don't preface the offer by telling him that his pets have died and then referring to them as "readily replaceable tangibles."

I could go on. But I'll just add that below Holly Winter's name there appeared her phone numbers: office, home, and cell. Hot come-on, huh?

CHAPTER 16

Early that evening, when the rain had stopped and Rowdy and Kimi were in the yard, Steve got through on his cell phone. By unfortunate coincidence, I'd taken advantage of the absence of the other dogs to let Sammy play with his Buster Cube, a one-dog toy if there ever was one, especially if even one of the dogs is a malamute. As perhaps I need to explain, the Buster Cube is a plastic box that you load with dry dog food or treats that it subsequently dispenses as the dog paws it, noses it, or, in Sammy's case, delivers massive whacks that send it noisily flying across the room. Anyway, Sammy was whamming the plastic toy across the tile of the kitchen floor when the phone rang, and since caller ID displayed Steve's cell number, I grabbed the wireless phone and took refuge in the living room.

"I'm so glad to hear your voice," I said before he'd had time to say a word. "I miss you. Are you okay?"

"Didn't you get my message? We're fine."

"That was days ago. Rowdy got a Group II on Saturday, and Sammy went Winners Dog. Steve, Teller is a mistake. He mixed up the dogs, and the handler he provided for Sammy was a dope. But the dogs looked good. I was proud of them. And it's always good to see Gabrielle."

"Did your father behave himself?"

"More or less. Not exactly. No. He could've been worse, I guess. And they left early this morning. Are you having fun?"

"Holly, I can't begin to tell you. The dogs are loving it. You should've come with us. No, you shouldn't. Except for the bugs, you'd love it. But they're pretty bad."

"I've had a lifetime's worth of black fly season in Maine. You've seen the scars. And I hate bug dope. It always ends up in my eyes."

"You've mentioned that once or twice," he said, meaning ten thousand times.

After that, I told Steve how much I loved and missed him, as I really did. I then intended to tell him about the murder, the whole Holly Winter identity business, the photo of the blue malamute, and so forth, but the damned inevitable intervened: with no warning, we lost the connection. I tried his number, got nowhere, waited for him to call back, tried his number again, and settled for leaving a short message in which I said nothing about the murder. The aborted call left me feeling cheated and unsettled. The sense of dissatisfaction lingered, and throughout the evening, I was restless and jumpy. In particular, my ears were sharply attuned to the sound of motorcycles passing by on Concord Avenue. Ridiculous! I was so used to the Concord Avenue traffic that it was background noise that ordinarily didn't register on me at all and had no business alarming me now. And why motorcycles? Damn! I'd sent the biker, Adam, in search of the other Holly Winter, but she'd been so unpleasant to me that the incident had slipped my mind and I'd neglected to ask her about him.

"He had nothing to do with us," I told Rowdy. "He was here by mistake."

Unless . . . unless the murdered woman had, in fact, begun to assume my identity? Or the identity of the other Holly Winter? Unless she'd passed herself off to Adam as one of us? *You have something for me.* That's what he'd said. I had a vivid memory of the view through the glass door into the kitchen where the body had lain. Someone, presumably the killer, had trashed the house in search of something. And found it? Failed to find it? And was still looking? *You have something for me.* The same thing he'd been seeking in Dr. Ho's house?

Whatever it was, I didn't have it. Furthermore, I knew nothing about it. At bedtime, I let go of what Rita would have called my "pointless obsessing" by surrounding myself with dogs. Rowdy slept on the bedroom floor under the air conditioner, which I'd turned on to provide white noise; Sammy was in his crate; and Kimi spent the night next to me on the bed, her spine to mine. It's possible, I suppose, that eight hours of close contact with Kimi's backbone cured me of my bout of spinelessness. For whatever reason, I awoke in the morning feeling calm but also feeling eager to do my part to figure out what the hell was going on, my part being, of course, to trace the identity of the blue malamute. Fortunately for Phyllis Hamilton, my eagerness did not prompt me to call her at seven a.m. when the dogs and I got up; since she'd been at the shows all weekend and had had a long drive back home to Pennsylvania, I decided to wait until at least eleven. At ten, however, just after I'd ordered a credit check, she called me.

When we'd exchanged greetings and

congratulations on the weekend's wins — Heart had gone Winners Bitch on Sunday — I filled Phyllis in on the circumstances surrounding my curiosity about the blue malamute.

Phyllis said, "Well, I can get you started. I knew there was something about her that was ringing a bell. I was thinking about her on the drive home. She has the look of the Snosquall dogs. But Minnie Wilcox stopped breeding . . . oh, it must be six years ago."

"I've heard the name," I said.

"And Debbie Alonso. You might have run into her. She's in Illinois."

"Crevasse?" I should perhaps point out that I was not asking whether Debbie Alonso had fallen into one. Rather, I was confirming that Crevasse was Debbie Alonso's kennel name.

"Yes."

"Is she still breeding?"

"No. You know, Holly, I've been thinking it over, and I think that maybe now I'm the only one actively breeding with blue in the lines. Not that I breed a lot. But maybe I'm the only one."

"You're the one everyone thinks of," I said. "Maybe because you show a lot. And win!"

"They both showed, but they weren't

141

around here. They were in Illinois. They bred some nice dogs. And then there was Graham Grant. You know about him."

"There was some kind of scandal. A couple of years ago? Some of his dogs ended up in rescue. That's all I remember."

Phyllis sighed in a way that expressed sadness and disgust. "Debbie took back the dogs he got from her, and I think she took Minnie's, too, but rescue helped with the ones he'd bred himself. You probably met him at the National in Massachusetts."

National: Alaskan Malamute National Speciality, an annual all-malamute dog show, the yearly gathering of our clan.

"I met hundreds of people there," I said. "I don't remember him."

"Oh, Grant was a charmer! And he had nice dogs. Well, he would. Snosquall and Crevasse lines."

"Did he belong to AMCA?" The Alaskan Malamute Club of America is our national breed club, membership in which is a sign of reputability. Among other things, you have to be sponsored by two established members, both of whom have to have known you for at least two years and one of whom has to have visited your house.

"Oh, yes. As far as anyone knew, he was a responsible breeder. Well, he *was,* I think, until his marriage fell apart, and he got into some kind of financial trouble. By the time people realized what was going on, his dogs were in terrible condition. Filthy. Starving. Debbie Alonso knows all about it. She was furious."

"What happened to Grant?"

"He disappeared, I think. And good riddance!"

The conversation left me with leads to pursue: I needed to get in touch with Minnie Wilcox and Debbie Alonso, and I also needed to find the malamute rescue people who'd taken in Grant's dogs. Had there been a blue female? If so, where had she gone? If I could find out who had adopted her, I'd be on my way to discovering a connection between the malamute in the photo and the unidentified woman who'd had the print in her possession. For all I knew, the murder victim herself had adopted the blue malamute, either from a breeder or from rescue. With luck, someone would recognize her description. Why had she had the photograph but not the dog? In examining the picture, I'd grown attached to the dog, but it was, of course, possible that she was dead. If so, the death had probably been recent; the police had found traces of dog hair on the woman's possessions. Of course, the hair might have come from a different dog. I made a mental note to ask Kevin for details. There were other possibilities. Maybe the unidentified woman had simply left her dog at home. Indeed, where was home? Or maybe . . .

Instead of trying to think out all possible scenarios, I got out my AMCA directory and looked up Minnie Wilcox and Debbie Alonso. In addition to listing names, kennel names, addresses, phone numbers, and e-mail addresses, the directory showed the month and year in which each person had become a member. Minnie Wilcox had joined about forty years ago; Debbie Alonso, twenty years ago. Some listings showed abbreviations for the services a member's kennel provided. The letter *P,* for example, meant that puppies were sometimes available, and *S* meant that stud service was available to approved bitches. Neither Minnie Wilcox nor Debbie Alonso listed her kennel as offering anything; as Phyllis had told me, neither was actively breeding.

I dialed Minnie Wilcox's number. A woman answered.

"My name is Holly Winter," I said. "Is Minnie Wilcox there, please?"

"Mom doesn't come to the phone very often these days," the woman said. "Can I help you?"

"Maybe. I'm trying to track down a blue malamute. I've just been talking to Phyllis Hamilton, and she thought maybe your mother could help."

"Phyllis doesn't know, I guess," the woman said. "Mom's been out of touch with everyone. She had a stroke about five years ago, and then her memory . . . her memory is failing. Well, worse than that. Basically, it's gone. She wouldn't be able to help you."

"I'm so sorry. I had no idea. I wouldn't have called." I paused. "Unless maybe you remember? There was a man named Graham Grant. He was a malamute breeder, and —"

"Sorry. I don't know. Mom hasn't had dogs since her stroke. She only had two, and a friend of hers took them. She moved in with me, and we don't have room."

"Do you remember who the friend was?"

"Debbie Alonso."

"I'll give her a call," I said.

When I tried, I got an answering machine and left a short message. After that, I wrote a long e-mail message to Elise Everett, who was active in the Illinois Alaskan Malamute Rescue Association and whom I knew because we both posted regularly to AMAL-L, the e-mail list maintained by the

Alaskan Malamute Assistance League. We also exchanged private e-mail and had friends in common. In fact, I had to think twice to remember that Elise and I had never actually met and had never even talked on the phone. Still, in e-mailing Elise, I had the sense of communicating with someone I knew fairly well. I gave Elise a short version of the whole story, mentioned Graham Grant, and provided a brief description of the unidentified woman. I also attached the photo of the blue malamute. Had Illinois Rescue taken in a blue female like this one? If so, who had adopted her? Could the adopter have been a woman matching the description?

Seconds after I'd sent the e-mail, my phone rang. I answered.

"Holly Winter?" a woman asked.

"Yes."

Her tone became oddly coy. "My name is Donna Yappel," she said. "Have you lost a dog?"

CHAPTER 17

Late on that same Monday morning, the other Holly Winter also makes phone calls. Data analyst that she is, she has winnowed down the list of 154 of us to just under 100. She begins with those of us in the eastern daylight time zone. Many of us are at work; it is, after all, Monday morning. When she reaches a machine or voice mail, she does not leave a message.

CHAPTER 18

"I'm trying to help someone find a lost Siberian husky. She isn't mine," I told Donna Yappel. "But I'm so glad to hear from you. Is she all right?"

"This is a boy," Donna Yappel said. "And he has your name on his tag. And your phone number. I think he's a boy. He's a boy isn't he?" She called out. "Yes, he's a boy. He's too big for a girl."

Although the call should have assured me that the dog — which dog? — was safe, my heart was pounding. Damn! No matter how careful you are — and I am very careful — any dog can get loose. Well, Sammy hadn't. At that moment, he wandered into the kitchen with Pink Piggy in his mouth. Rowdy. Damn it all! He and Kimi were in the yard, or that's where they were supposed to be, and that yard was close to what's known as Malcatraz: escape-proof containment for malamutes. My house formed one wall of the yard. Opposite it was the long, narrow little building at the actual corner of Appleton Street and Concord Avenue that housed a diminutive shop. Its brick wall was my wall, too, and the dogs couldn't possibly have climbed it. The wooden fences at the front and back of the yard were six feet high, and to prevent the dogs from digging under, I'd buried chicken wire and poured in enough concrete to provide a solid foundation for a substantial house. The gate to the driveway was as high as the fence. It had two latches, both secured with snap bolts, and a sturdy lock. My suspicions fell on Kimi, the most vigorous digger in our pack. If Rowdy had escaped and been found, then Kimi was loose.

"I'll be right back!" After shouting into the phone and dropping it on the counter, I ran to the door that leads to the yard, threw it open, and was in equal parts amazed and relieved to see Rowdy and Kimi curled up on the mulch taking midmorning naps. I closed the door, caught my breath, and returned to the phone. "My dogs are here," I said. "All three of them. We have two more, but they're both on a canoe trip with my husband in Minnesota. I don't know what to say."

"You *are* Holly Winter?"

149

"Yes, but —"

"His tag has your name and this number, and if you don't want your dog —"

"It isn't that. It isn't that at all. But maybe I'd better take a look at the dog. Where are you?"

The address Donna Yappel gave me was in Lexington, which is, of course, famous as one of Paul Revere's principal destinations. The green in the center has a minuteman statue, and on Patriots' Day, authentically costumed men reenact the Battle of Lexington. It's a pretty town, with houses that date to the Revolutionary War and also with large neighborhoods of ranch houses and such that date to the years just after World War II. The Yappels lived on a street of what must originally have been almost identical split-level houses. Over time, as Lexington real estate values had increased, owners had built upward and outward, and what had started out as modest tract housing had become prosperous and individualized. Donna Yappel's house, for instance, was a split-level with large additions on either side, one with big windows, the other with walls made entirely of glass. Natural wood siding and timbers were everywhere, and the wide steps to the front door were made of three or four different kinds of stone.

Instead of a lawn and conventional shrubbery, the grounds were landscaped with thickly planted perennials, low evergreens, and what I was surprised to recognize as highbush and lowbush blueberries. In spite of the proximity of neighboring houses, the place had the feel of a luxurious lodge in a wooded resort.

When I rang the bell, I had the vivid fantasy that I'd be greeted by the barking of small dogs. Yappel? People with canine names are greatly overrepresented among dog lovers of every variety, from AKC judges like Mrs. Woofenden to pet owners named Fox, Basset, Baylor, Collier, Howland, and, I assumed, Yappel. Are these people drawn to dogs because of a sense of natural affinity? Are dog-loving women compelled to marry and take the names of men called Wolf, Ladd, and Barker? Life's little mysteries! In any case, although the bell chimed, the pack of terriers failed to show up. The woman who answered the door, Donna Yappel, looked like a grandmother in a children's book. Her silver hair was swept up in a loose knot on her head, and it was easy to see that when she sat down, she'd have a comfy lap.

When she'd ushered me into a spacious hallway filled with gigantic houseplants, I said, "Thank you for calling. I have no idea what's going on, but we'll find out. All of my own dogs are definitely accounted for. I am mystified."

In a guilt-inducing tone, she said, "He is a very sweet dog. Very friendly. And he was starving, poor thing." As she spoke, her eyes darted down and then left and right, as if she were checking to see whether something was there. "Donald!" she called. "Donald!"

As you'll have guessed, I assumed that Donald was the little terrier who'd mysteriously failed to herald my arrival and whose presence Donna Yappel had been seeking when she'd scanned the floor.

"The husky is in the yard," she said to me as I followed her to what proved to be a large kitchen with stainless-steel appliances, granite counters, and cherry cabinets and woodwork. "Donald! Oh, there you are!"

I nearly gasped. My sense that Donna Yappel owned a terrier turned out to be almost correct. The incorrect part was this: Donna Yappel didn't own a dog; rather, she was married to one, and a handsome one at that. His breed was unmistakable. Donald Yappel was an Irish terrier. His hair and his neatly trimmed beard were wheaten and were, as the AKC standard says, "dense and wiry in texture." His head was long, his skull was flat, and his eyes were not only dark brown but, and again I quote, "full of life, fire, and intelligence, showing an intense expression."

"This is Donald," she said. "My husband."

Restraining the impulse to stroke his shoulder, I said, "I'm Holly Winter." With heartfelt sincerity, I added, "Pleased to meet you."

His eyes crackling, Donald said, "Pleased to meet you, too, now that you've decided to take responsibility for your dog."

I know when to quit. "How did you happen to find him?" I asked.

"Oh, he's been around for a couple of days," Donna said, "but it was only this morning that he showed up on our doorstep."

"Starving," Donald said pointedly.

"At first, I was a little afraid of him because of his size, but Donald lured him into the yard, and once he was there, we saw how friendly he is. He's quite the clown! There, you see! He's doing it right now!"

Donna Yappel pointed to a glass door eerily like the one at Dr. Ho's house. This door, however, gave me a view radically different from the one I'd had there. Just on the other side of the glass, lying on her back on a teak deck, waving her big white snowshoe paws in the air, eyeing the three of us, and begging for a belly rub, was a distinctly female Alaskan malamute. Her color was unusual. Indeed, it was the rarest color in the breed: blue. She looked just like her picture. I still had no idea where the blue malamute in the photo had come from, and I had no idea who she was, but I knew for certain where she'd gone and knew that she was right in front of me.

I slid the door open, stepped onto the deck, and rubbed her white tummy. "We meet at last," I said. Whispering so that the Yappels wouldn't hear me, I added, "You're safe now. You're with one of your own."

CHAPTER 19

As a rescue volunteer, I've had it drummed into me that I'm to do everything by the book, which is to say, according to the procedures established by Betty Burley, the founder of our organization. "Leave a paper trail," Betty is always reminding me, by which she means, among other things, that whenever an owner or a shelter surrenders a dog to us, I have to get a signed release stating, in brief, that the signer has the right to turn the dog over to us and that the dog is now ours. The Yappels, however, didn't own the blue malamute. Furthermore, she wasn't being surrendered to our organization, was she? Since she'd been found in Lexington, the proper agency to take possession of her was probably the local animal-control department, which would be required to hold her for a week or ten days or some such period of time to give her owner a chance to claim her. On the other hand, since she could be considered evidence in a homicide, the Cambridge Police Department and any county and state agencies involved in the murder investigation must have a claim on her, too. Betty Burley absolutely hated any ambiguity about ownership. In particular, she had what amounted to a cop's loathing of any domestic disturbance. If I took in a dog because of a divorce or separation, I was under orders to get a signed release of ownership from the dog's actual owner or owners and never to take one partner's word for it that the other partner also wanted to be rid of the dog. Without calling Betty, I hurriedly decided that in the absence of anyone with a clear legal claim to the blue malamute, she temporarily belonged to me. I didn't even bother to ask the Yappels to sign any kind of release form. For one thing, Donald Yappel, being an Irish terrier, would've given me a spirited argument about any such request. For another, both Donald and Donna were still convinced that the dog they'd found had been mine to begin with.

I could hardly blame them. When I fastened the leash I'd brought with me to her collar, I examined her tags. One was exactly what Donna Yappel had described, an ID tag that bore my name and phone number.

It also gave my address. Unlike the ID tags on my own dogs, it did not have my cell number. As Donna hadn't mentioned, it was the sort of engraved tag that you can have made by machine while you wait at kennel-supply shops, and it looked brand-new. The other tag, in contrast, showed heavy wear. It was a rabies tag issued by Steve's clinic, certainly a rabies tag issued to some other dog. If anyone at the clinic had seen a malamute, and especially a blue malamute, Steve would have known and would definitely have told me. I was headed for the clinic, anyway. When I got there, I'd examine the tag and have someone look up its number.

One other thing that I noticed immediately: the rolled leather collar. Malamute breeders whose dogs live mainly in kennels sometimes leave their dogs without collars unless the dogs are going somewhere, in part to avoid freak accidents in which dogs strangle and in part to avoid leaving collar marks in the dogs' coats. Flat buckle collars, in particular, mash down the coat and can even damage it. Consequently, many of us — and I use *us* in the obnoxious sense, meaning those of us in the knowledgeable elite — use rolled leather collars. To the best of my recollection, I'd never seen one on a rescue malamute surrendered by an owner or turned over by a shelter. Still, every pet shop and kennel-supply store in the country sold rolled leather collars. I reminded myself not to make more of the collar than it might actually mean.

"Let's go, young lady," I said. "Ride in the car, Miss Blue?" I was following one of Betty Burley's rules, and a good one: there are no nameless dogs. If you don't know the dog's name, make one up.

To my embarrassment, the combination of the name and Miss Blue's eagerness to go with me reinforced the Yappels' conviction that she belonged to me. In my defense, I informed them that she was a female rather than the male they'd taken her to be, but my assertion only made matters worse by seeming to prove that I had intimate knowledge of a dog I was trying to disown. The Yappels' opinion of me didn't matter. I gave up, thanked them, and led Miss Blue to Steve's van.

"The same thing happens to my Kimi all the time," I told Miss Blue as I opened the side door of the van. "She rolls over on her back, and half the world looks at her and still thinks that since she's big and strong, she has to be a boy. Don't let it bother you."

Steve's van held five big crates, one for

each of our dogs. We shifted crates around from Steve's van to my Blazer to the house fairly often. At the moment, the one just behind the driver's seat was a big Central Metal wire crate. Since it occupied what Rowdy considered to be the prime location in the van, it was his favorite. If he played Monopoly, he'd go for Boardwalk and Park Place. If I played with him, I'd probably let him win. Or watch him trounce me? Yes, who says that I don't already? He usually rides where he wants to ride. Anyway, some dogs have a strong preference either for a wire crate or for an opaque, airline-approved crate of the Vari Kennel type. If Miss Blue proved reluctant to enter Rowdy's crate, I'd try one of the Vari Kennels. If she balked at both, I'd rethink my plans. I hate driving with a dog loose in a vehicle. If there's an accident, the dog can be thrown against the windshield. If you and the dog are really unlucky, he can collide with you. A great many pets, however, are used to riding loose and are reluctant to enter a crate. The lure of food tossed into the depths of safety sometimes works. And sometimes fails. Miss Blue was easy. She knew what a crate was. As I opened Rowdy's, I was prepared to offer the enticement of liver treats from my never-empty pockets, but she popped right in and got her treat as a reward, and on the drive to Cambridge, she was quiet and still.

I went directly to Steve's clinic. Even though he's my husband, I probably should have called first, but I won't use my cell while I'm behind the wheel. I grew up in Maine. That's probably why I'll never make it as a Boston driver. I refrain from the popular local custom of reading while driving; I never apply mascara while negotiating a crowded traffic circle; I don't start manicuring my nails at one traffic light and have the polish on by the time I reach the next; and even when I'm hard up against a deadline, I refuse to keep my notebook computer open on the front passenger seat to allow me to steer with my left hand while typing with my right. I could've pulled over to make the call, but people would've given me funny looks and maybe even called the police to report me for a grossly deviant violation of the rules of the Greater Boston road. For careful driving around here, you're likely to lose your license. Anyway, all I intended to do at the clinic was to borrow an exam room and then either requisition kennel space for Miss Blue or crate her upstairs in what used to be Steve's apartment.

As it turned out, one of Steve's colleagues

was free. Dr. Zoe Wang-Lopez had worked for him for only about six months, but his entire staff and clientele liked her, and we hoped that she'd stay. Her credentials were great: she'd graduated from Cornell Veterinary School a few years ago and had spent the time after that at Boston's famous Angell Animal Medical Center. During her time at Angell, Dr. Zoe Wang fell in love, cut off all but a half inch of her hair, swore off skirts, hyphenated her name to reflect her life partnership with Angela Lopez, and moved across the Charles River to diversity-friendly Cambridge, a sanctuary city in which Angela, who'd been born in Mexico, wouldn't have to worry about her immigration status. Zoe's parents had cut her off almost completely but had been unable to sever the tie between Zoe and her trust fund, so she'd bought a house in East Cambridge, where she and Angela lived with the family they'd created. It consisted of two lively pit bull terriers and a Siamese cat that had bitten five people and, in my opinion, had a taste for human blood.

So, only about a half hour after I'd left the Yappels', Miss Blue was standing on the linoleum in one of Steve's small examining rooms, and Dr. Zoe Wang-Lopez was peering into her ears and speaking to her in soft, serious tones. "Well, you are young. One and a half? Two? Your eyes are clear. You have full dentition. Seventy-nine pounds is four pounds on the plump side. Let's settle for having you lose three, okay, young lady? Your heart rate says that you're not feeling stressed. No vet phobia, huh? That's good news."

Zoe was right. The dog I'd christened Miss Blue was gently wagging her tail over her back. Her ears were neither flat nor hyperalert, and her expression was relaxed and happy. Although I remained mystified about her identity, she knew exactly who she was and was obviously content to be herself.

"Do you have a spay scar?" Zoe asked her. "Not that I can find, but you never know for sure, do you? Not unless . . . Would you like an ultrasound, young lady?"

As Zoe Wang-Lopez continued to educate Miss Blue about her state of health and to pose questions that Miss Blue couldn't answer, I made mental notes. Miss Blue's coat showed clear evidence that, until recently, she'd received regular grooming. Malamutes, of course, have a double coat: a coarse, water-repellant guard coat covers the dense, woolly undercoat. In winter, I dress the same way by wearing a parka or a windbreaker over Polartec or silk longjohns that I routinely remove and wash. Malamute undercoat also renews itself in the sense that the dog sheds and that new hair grows in, but if the old undercoat is not thoroughly removed, it can form a dense layer of dead hair and dirt that looks and sometimes smells like an ugly, stinky old carpet pad. Once that layer gets wet, the dirt and dampness trapped against the dog's warm skin provide an excellent environment for fungal and bacterial growth and for the development of "hot spots," as they are known, patches of irritation that the dog feels compelled to scratch and lick. Ugh. Enough said. And the dog looks lousy, too. The point is that not every owner of a double-coated breed knows how to remove the dead hair. If you simply run a brush over the dog, you are brushing only the surface, that is, the guard coat. Ideally, you blast with a powerful dryer while brushing against the direction of growth, but you can also use an undercoat rake, and you can "line brush" and "line comb," that is, part the coat and work on one small section at a time to brush or comb from the skin out. Miss Blue was fortunate to lack the layer of dead undercoat. Therefore, her owner had either had her groomed by a diligent professional or had done a good job at home. Furthermore, although her nails hadn't been trimmed within the last week or two, they weren't overgrown.

The door to the exam room swung open, and a vet tech named Alvin stuck his head in. "Kimi's rabies tag," he said. "Her old one."

"Thank you," I said. "Zoe, could we scan for a microchip?"

Leaving momentous pauses between her words, Zoe said, "Who . . . are . . . you . . . Miss Blue?"

The scanner failed to answer the question. Microchips, which are, of course, tiny ID devices, are usually injected at the base of the neck, about where the neck meets the back, but microchips can migrate. Zoe checked Miss Blue's throat and chest and kept looking, but no number appeared on the scanner. In searching for a spay scar, she'd already looked for a tattoo and found none. The absence of permanent ID meant nothing. It's not all that easy to find someone to do a really clear tattoo on a dog. Some owners don't trust microchip technology. A lot of people intend to have dogs chipped and never get around to it. And Miss Blue did, after all, have a collar and tags, albeit tags that didn't belong on her. I'd hoped that a close examination of her collar might yield information, but the collar was not, to my disappointment, a luxurious and expensive one that I might have been able to trace to a particular retailer. It was nothing but a plain rolled-leather collar that I suspected was Miss Blue's own. It wasn't brand new, and the leather showed no marks to indicate that it had been used on a dog with a neck larger or smaller than Miss Blue's.

"Zoe, do you think there's any chance that she's pregnant?" I asked.

"Hey, there's always a chance. You been up to anything, young lady? No, seriously, I'm not finding anything."

"Good." A few years earlier, my rescue group had sent an adopter directly to a shelter in Maine where there'd been a female malamute in need of a home, a spayed female, or so everyone had believed. Soon after the adopter got home with her dog, she found herself in possession of twice what she'd intended: one adult malamute and one newborn puppy. Fortunately, she'd been overjoyed as well as surprised. Good sportsmanship is highly valued in all spheres of the dog world, including rescue. "Let's hold off on an ultrasound. And on her shots," I said. "It's possible that I'll find out where she belongs and get her vet records."

"You leaving her here?"

"Kimi wouldn't give her a warm welcome. And let's check a stool sample and keep an eye on her. She could be incubating something. But I'll be back tomorrow and give her some play time. Okay, Miss Blue? You're safe here. I know you'll be a good girl."

After I'd led Miss Blue to the waiting room, as I was hanging around to find a vet tech to take her, I reached into my pocket for a treat and tried baiting her as I'd have done in the show ring. She had no idea what I wanted. On the other hand, she sat on command, albeit slowly. In the conformation ring, it's undesirable to have a dog sit, so dogs intended only for the show ring sometimes don't know the command. When I returned, I'd try a few obedience commands, but the world of malamute obedience was so small that if she'd been actively shown in that sport, I'd probably have heard of her. But she'd had some pet training. So far, she seemed to be housebroken. She walked quite well on leash. She hadn't jumped on anyone.

So, although she was show quality, she wasn't an experienced show dog. The observation meant nothing. I'd heard experts say that the very best dogs weren't in the show ring but in pet owners' backyards. But she had a malamute-savvy owner, one who'd bought a correct collar and who'd known how to groom her. The owner had used a crate. Miss Blue was friendly, and even in the potentially stressful situation of a vet visit, she'd remained happy and relaxed. Someone had spent time with her and had taken her to new places. Someone had made sure that she was wearing identification; someone had wanted to be sure that if Miss Blue got loose and was found, a responsible person would be informed. I, of course, was that responsible person.

CHAPTER 20

"Kevin, relax," I said as he hesitated outside Mr. Bartley's Burger Cottage, where we'd arranged to meet. "What do you think they're going to do? Ask for Harvard ID? And not let us in if we don't have it? It's your kind of food. And when Jennifer gets back, you're going to be eating bok choy and tofu again."

"I've been here before," Kevin declared.

"And you loved it." I amended the statement. "You loved the food."

He reluctantly nodded in agreement and held the door open for me. It was early on that same Monday evening. With Steve and Jennifer both out of town, Kevin and I were once again having dinner together. Bartley's was my choice. I knew that Kevin would object. It's on Mass. Ave. near the corner of Bow Street, just across from Harvard Yard, and in its own way it's as Harvardian as University Hall, Widener Library, and the

Fogg Art Museum, its own way being noisy, greasy, and crowded. What makes it Harvardian is the clientele, which consists principally, although not exclusively, of students. Alumni and alumnae show up, too, as do members of the faculty and administration eager for real food. No healthy person leaves Bartley's hungry. That's one reason it's my kind of place. The other is that it helps to cure my homesickness for Moody's Diner on Route 1 in Waldoboro, Maine, which, like Helen's Restaurant in Machias, serves up traditional Maine fare, the defining ingredient of which is neither lobsters nor blueberries but good old dietary fat. If Maine tourist bureaus were honest about the nature of real Maine food, all of these lobster festivals and blueberry festivals would be subsumed by a single gigantic Annual Maine Grease Festival. I'd attend. It doesn't yet exist, alas. In the meantime, there's Bartley's.

Bartley's being the popular place it justifiably is, it was crowded. Even if there'd been no customers, it would've been hard for Kevin to make his way to the back because the tables were so close together. Since it took us a while to maneuver through the almost nonexistent aisles, Kevin had a chance to read the offerings chalked on the big blackboard and to observe the platefuls of food the servers were carrying, so by the time we were seated, with Kevin mashed in a corner, he'd quit looking uneasy. The menus presented to us by a hurried, hot-looking waiter listed all sorts of sandwiches named for celebrities and a variety of other items not on the blackboard, but Kevin ordered two burgers with American cheese, a side of french fries, a side of onion rings, and a Coke, and I asked for a mozzarella burger and a ginger ale.

Looking around and taking note of the multiracial clientele, Kevin said, "Ethnic. Sign of a good restaurant. But geez, some of these kids are wicked thin. Give 'em some time in America, and we'll build 'em up." He turned his attention to me. "So what's going on?"

"A case of canine identity theft," I said somewhat melodramatically. "I have the blue malamute. She was found wandering in Lexington. She's at Steve's clinic. Kevin, this is the dog in the picture. No question."

"Tags?"

"That's the strange thing, Kevin. That's the really peculiar thing. Yes, she has tags. Two. One is a new ID tag with my name, my address, and my phone number. The other is Kimi's old rabies tag. Kimi had a rabies shot, and when I put the new tag on her collar, I threw out the old one. The new ID tag on the dog must've come from a machine at one of the pet-supply places, but Kimi's rabies tag came from my trash. Just like my bills and bank statements and stuff. Kimi got her rabies shot before Steve left, and that's when I threw out the old tag. But the point is that that woman wasn't just preparing to steal my identity. And the other Holly Winter's, of course. *Preparing* is the right word, by the way. I checked my credit. It's fine. Anyway, while she was gathering information on us, she was also stealing Kimi's identity for her dog."

"The dog wasn't living there," Kevin said. "At Dr. Ho's. There was dog hair, consistent with a malamute, by the way, but it was on her clothes, stuff like that. Small quantities. Not all over the place. Not like at your house."

"I beg your pardon! We own two Dyson vacuum cleaners, and I vacuum all the time."

Let me pause here for a short commercial break. A household with three Alaskan malamutes, a German shepherd, a pointer, and a cat constitutes a tough test for a vacuum cleaner. Dyson doesn't just pass the test; it gets an A plus. Every other brand fails.

I said, "Anyway, I don't know how long the dog was loose. The people in Lexington said that she'd been around for a few days, but that's just in their neighborhood. And they weren't very observant. They thought she was a male. Do you know when this woman got to Cambridge? Or when she started living at Dr. Ho's?"

"August twenty-ninth, give or take. That was a Tuesday. That's when he took off. She wasn't there on August twenty-seventh. Sunday. That was when his house sitter backed out. The guy called him Sunday morning. Dr. Ho had some friends there for one of these brunches, and the guy who was supposed to house-sit called while they were there. Ho was wicked pissed. Because of the fish."

"Understandably. Two days' notice? Why did the house sitter back out? Is there any chance that this woman somehow arranged —"

Our waiter appeared with Kevin's burgers and soon reappeared with mine and with large platters of fries and onion rings that had to go directly between Kevin's plate and mine because there was nowhere else for them on the little table. Kevin is good about sharing.

"The house sitter got offered a job in a chemistry lab at Harvard. We checked it out. This is a Harvard kid who got a better job and didn't want to be bothered doing this one. No more to it. No connection with anyone else."

"Well, if Dr. Ho had had any sense, he'd've hired a vet tech to feed the fish. Or a pet-sitting service."

"His friends say he didn't want the house empty. That was then. Yeah, he'd've been better off."

"Any luck reaching him?"

"Not directly. Someone left a message at some place he's supposed to get to on Wednesday or Thursday."

"His friends. Did they know anything about the woman?"

Kevin was chewing on a mouthful of cheeseburger. Eventually, he said, "Barfly. Huh. Sushi barfly, like you heard. That's what they say."

"Loaves and Fishes," I said.

"Help yourself to fries and onion rings."

"Thank you. I have been."

"No kidding?" Kevin grinned. "Not bad. Good."

"Real food. Any possibility that Dr. Ho met her somewhere else? That he'd known her before?"

"Different types."

I refrained from pointing out to Kevin that he and I were, too.

"She had some of these romance what-chamacallits, soft porn only not quite. Movie star magazines."

"No one has suggested that he was seeking intellectual companionship. But I gather that he made a habit of it."

"That's what the neighbors say, but they hadn't seen this one before."

"I wonder what she was doing at Loaves and Fishes. Dr. Ho lives right near there, and lots of people shop there. I do. Your mother does. And so did Dr. Ho. And maybe this woman did, too. But another possibility is that . . . Look, if you're driving to Cambridge or heading toward Boston on Route 2, the highway part of Route 2 ends, you pass the Alewife T station, and then you come to all those shops on both sides of the street. If you've been on highways, Route 95 or 495, and then Route 2, then those stores, including Loaves and Fishes, are an obvious place to stop. For food. Or a bathroom. And, of course, it's a short walk from the Alewife T station, too. Anyway, just a thought. Kevin, when was she killed? Do you know?"

"Yeah. Not to the minute. But that Tuesday before you found her. September fifth. That evening. Night. That's an estimate. These guys never want to sound sure of themselves in case it turns out they're wrong."

"No one heard a shot?"

"It's not the quietest neighborhood."

"People weren't outside? It couldn't have been raining. We had rain the day I found her, but all the plants were wilted. That was Thursday, so there couldn't have been much rain on Tuesday. But if she was shot during the night . . . someone would've heard. Those houses are close together. Maybe when people were watching TV? She must've been killed where I found her, in the kitchen, and that's at the back of the house. Most of those houses have living rooms at the front, near the street. If it was during prime time, the neighbors might've been in their living rooms." Thinking of Francie's mention of her media-free preschool, I added, "Except that some of them may not have been watching TV. But what do I know? The neighbors could have been anywhere. Out. Studying. Reading. Watching shoot-'em-up movies. Anything. What was the weapon?"

"Smith and Wesson .22/.32 Kit Gun.

They're pretty sure."

That's a revolver. "Huh. My father has one. So does practically everyone else in Maine. But Buck's is a classic. It's a Model 63. Stainless. They aren't made anymore. The stainless was replaced by, uh, aluminum, I think. I used to use it for target practice."

"Firing .22 short."

"Are you asking me? Or telling me? Yes, because my mother hated the sound of gunshots, and compared with larger calibers . . ." I caught on. "And that's one reason —"

"Plus contact shooting," Kevin said. "Pressed the muzzle right up against her."

"To muffle the sound. So the result would've been . . . well, far from silent. But easy enough to mistake for a car backfiring. Or some other city noise."

On the subject of noise level, as I've mentioned, the tables at Bartley's were close together, and by now every single seat was taken. The other customers were talking as well as eating, the waiters and cooks weren't exactly keeping their voices down, and cooking sounds added to the din. Because the background noise was loud and because our table was in a corner, with Kevin against a wall, I hadn't given a thought to being overheard by nearby customers, who were preoccupied with one another, but Kevin and I hadn't been having the typical Harvard Square conversation about dissertations, classes, professors, books, papers, and films.

"Five bullets," Kevin said. "Lodged in her. That's a low-penetration bullet."

At the table next to ours sat a young couple. At a guess, they were freshmen or sophomores, the woman tiny and pale, with light hair in a low ponytail, the man dark and serious, all in khaki. Woman. Man. The language of Cambridge! Truth: a girl and boy. Anyway, they kept darting glances at us, leaning their heads in over the platter of french fries that occupied the center of their table, whispering in each other's ears, and sitting back with sour expressions on their faces. The cause of the pickle faces was not, I might mention, Bartley's pickles, which are crisp, flavorful, and altogether outstanding.

"Kevin," I said, "this conversation is a little graphic for our neighbors."

Two seconds after I'd spoken, I realized that Kevin had already observed the couple and assessed their reaction. Practically before I'd finished speaking, he extended his gigantic right hand to the girl, shook it vigorously, and then repeated the act with the boy while saying, "Kevin Dennehy. Cambridge Police Department." A big, terrifying grin appeared on his massive face.

"P-p-pleased to meet you," said the girl. "We didn't mean to —"

"Violence," said Kevin. "Enough to rob you of your appetite." This from someone who had just devoured two seven-ounce hamburgers topped with cheese and at least half of the fries and onion rings! "Line of duty," he proclaimed solemnly. With that, he turned his attention back to the remaining food, thus leaving me the task of changing the subject.

"The dog," I said. "Here's what I can tell you about her." I summarized my observations concerning the state of Miss Blue's coat and nails, the choice of a rolled-leather collar, her readiness to enter a crate in the van, and so forth. "So," I concluded, "none of these things alone means much, but the combination suggests a knowledgeable owner. I don't think that Miss Blue has been spayed. Miss Blue. That's what I'm calling her for the moment. Anyway, it's remotely possible that we just can't see a scar. One of the vets looked, and she couldn't find one, but you can't necessarily. For instance, if Miss Blue was spayed very early, say at six weeks, there might not be a visible scar. But it's possible that someone wanted to leave open the option of showing her and maybe breeding her."

"Rare blue malamutes," Kevin said.

"I don't think there'd be much market for them. Color doesn't matter, really. It's just a matter of personal preference. Someone out to make money might be able to create a market for all-white malamutes. But not blue. Most people don't even know what it is when they see it. A naive puppy buyer who wants a supposedly rare malamute is going to want one that basically deviates a lot from the standard. A giant malamute. Or a long-haired malamute. A woolly, those are called. They crop up in careful breedings, but good breeders don't deliberately breed them. Blue just isn't different enough from gray to be a major selling point to the general public. No, her color wouldn't be a reason to breed her. Her quality might. Her ears are a little big, but that's trivial. Her lines, whatever they are. Someone might want to breed for that. If her hips are good. Her eyes. But I'm guessing. I still don't know who she is."

"Stolen?"

"Probably not. If she were stolen, I'd probably have heard by now. There'd probably have been something on one of the malamute lists. But I can't rule that out. And I'm waiting to hear from a few people. Anyway, that's all I know. Or all I can guess. Do you know any more about Adam? The Harley rider."

"No, but I've been thinking about him. She was more his type than you are."

"I'm flattered. Except that he wasn't exactly . . . the stereotype of bikers? There are a lot of bikers who don't fit it. And the Harley must've been far from cheap. Look, Kevin, just in Cambridge there are probably plenty of doctors and lawyers who've spent their lives doing exactly what their parents wanted them to do and who've made a lot of money and who decide that deep in their souls lurks James Dean or the young Marlon Brando. Che Guevara. So, they buy Harleys. Or classic Nortons. Triumphs. Not that Adam struck me as that type. But if what you're thinking is some stereotype of motorcycle gangs, he didn't fit that, either. No tattoos that I saw. No —" I broke off. Contemplating the remains of the fries and onion rings and savoring the miasma of Bartley's, I reluctantly said, "No grease."

"I got a job for you," Kevin said. "Home-work. Look on the Web and see if you can find a picture of the bike. If you do, print it out. Get me the model."

"I'll try. I think I'll recognize it." I paused. "Kevin, one other thing about the woman. And the dog. That ID tag? Kevin, she had that made, and she put it on the dog."

"Someone did."

"Okay, someone did. But the point is the same. Whoever put my name and my contact information on the tag wanted to make sure that if the dog got lost, as she did, or got in some kind of trouble, I'd be the person who was called about her. If you just wanted a tag, any old tag, you could invent a name and an address and a phone number. Or use your own, of course. Or pick a person at random. But when it comes to malamutes, I'm not just anyone. I'm active in malamute rescue, I belong to our national breed club, I'm on all the e-mail lists about malamutes, I show my dogs, and so on. In my column and in my articles, I write about malamutes all the time, my malamutes, other people's malamutes, rescue malamutes, malamute history, malamute health, you name it. Do a Web search looking for me, and half of what you'll find will be about malamutes. So, what I think is that whoever had that tag made and put it on the dog, on Miss Blue, was someone who knew about me and who cared about the dog. Yes, in a way, the tags were canine identity theft, but Kimi doesn't have credit cards to steal or bank accounts to empty. She doesn't have a Social Security number. The point wasn't Kimi. The point was that I'm someone you could count on to do everything possible to help that dog. Why choose me? Because someone loved Miss Blue. And that's the real point of the canine identity theft. Someone loved her. Someone loved her enough to pass her off, even briefly, as my dog."

CHAPTER 21

Holly Winter and her mother make their way along Quincy Street, reach the intersection with Mass. Ave., pause to wait for a break in the traffic, and cross at the mother's pace, which is slow. The mother, who is short and plump, is not, of course, my mother, Marissa, who was tallish, athletic, and notably swift of foot. The major difference between our mothers is, however, the difference between life and death: whereas the other Holly's mother is alive, mine died a long time ago. If it had been my mother's ghost and me who walked along Quincy Street and crossed Mass. Ave., it's likely that we'd have been heading to Mr. Bartley's Burger Cottage. I inherited my healthy appetite from both parents, but my metabolism is Marissa's. When she used to take me to Harvard Square, we sometimes ate at Bartley's, where she gave as little thought to calories as I do. In contrast to the other

Holly Winter's mother, mine was energetic. As she used to say, "You can't work as hard as I do if you don't eat."

The other Holly Winter and her mother are walking, albeit slowly, toward a Thai restaurant that my mother would have hated. Steve loves the place, mainly because its menu items show little icons of peppers to indicate the spiciness or blandness of dishes. He is thus able to order and devour concoctions so blisteringly hot that they'd send me to the hospital. My mother hated hot peppers. In fact, Yankee that she was, she mistrusted even ordinary black pepper and used it sparingly, mainly as one of her rare concessions to the wants of other people. Or, I might add, the wants of dogs. Marissa met people's needs, and she more than met the needs of our golden retrievers, but needs are not wants, are they? Well, maybe sometimes they are.

"I need you to take my arm," says the mother. "It's so confusing. I don't know how you manage to find your way around."

"It's perfectly simple," says Holly impatiently. "And we don't have far to go."

"This one must be good," says the mother as Holly leads her around the line on the sidewalk in front of Bartley's. "We could go here. What is it we're having? Siamese food?"

"Thai." She is about to say more when she catches sight of a couple emerging from the Harvard Square landmark that she wrongfully dismisses as a greasy spoon. As a statistician, she fully understands that statistical correlation does not imply causation. There is, however, nothing statistical about the association she is now observing. Rather, what she sees is a social association, the coming together of a Cambridge police lieutenant and a woman named Holly Winter, another Holly Winter, a Holly Winter who differs from herself in radical and suspect ways.

CHAPTER 22

As I maneuvered Steve's van out of a Harvard Square parking garage built for compacts and as I drove home, I couldn't help wondering what the other Holly Winter had made of seeing me with Kevin, or maybe what she had made of seeing Kevin with me. She knew who we were, at least in a superficial sense. Kevin had questioned her, and she'd paid a visit to my house. She'd obviously recognized us. No one ever misses Kevin. He's a great big man with red hair, and although I don't exactly believe in auras or energy fields, Kevin exudes such a strong sense of presence that it would be a gross understatement to say that he stands out in a crowd. The line outside Bartley's had consisted mainly of late-adolescent students and of Harvardian adults with more brains than brawn. In that particular crowd, Kevin had looked like a woolly mammoth in a flock of sheep. I, perhaps, stood out as the sheepdog. In any case, there'd been no question about whether we were together. Kevin may be a mammoth, but he's a gentlemanly one: he'd taken my arm as he'd made a path for us through the line. Catching sight of us, Holly Winter had visibly startled. In reality, Kevin and I were friends and next-door neighbors, but she must have seen only a Cambridge cop investigating the death of the woman who'd been stealing her identity and the woman who shared her name, the name that had been stolen, the same woman who had found the body of the would-be identity thief. It occurred to me that if the other Holly Winter searched the Web for information about Kevin and about me, she'd find nothing about our friendship. Furthermore, although Kevin lives next door to me, his mother is the one who owns the house, and the phone there is in her name; and whereas I'm listed as living on Concord Avenue, the Dennehys' address is on Appleton Street. If the other Holly searched only for the Cambridge address of Kevin Dennehy, she might well fail to discover that we lived next door to each other. For all I knew, Cambridge had multiple Kevin Dennehys as well as multiple Holly Winters. When it comes to names, Greater Boston is as Irish as Dublin. Consequently, she might decide that my Kevin was some other Kevin Dennehy who lived nowhere near me.

When I arrived home, it was only seven thirty. Kevin eats early, and I eat anytime, as is indicative of our positions on the town-gown continuum: town has supper at five or five thirty, gown has dinner at seven thirty or eight, and I eat when the people I'm with want to eat or, if I'm alone, whenever it suits me. The dogs are evidently town rather than gown. To maintain flexibility in my own schedule, I avoid feeding them at exactly the same time every day, but they nonetheless remain convinced that five o'clock means food. Consequently, I'd fed them before leaving for the Square.

When I returned, I put Rowdy and Kimi outside in the yard and gave Sammy and Tracker, my cat, some house time. Neither Rowdy nor Kimi had been raised with cats, and although I'd made some slight progress in teaching them to remain calm in Tracker's presence, I'd had to accept my limits as a trainer. Rightly is it said that dogs build character! Malamutes specialize in instilling in their owners a deep sense of humility. Rowdy and Kimi had learned to exhibit calm behavior when Tracker was on top of the refrigerator or otherwise out of their reach, but it would never be safe to have her loose with either one alone, never mind both. Sammy, however, had known Tracker since he was a little puppy. I wouldn't have trusted him with her outdoors, but when the two had the run of the house, he largely ignored her. Because of the dogs, Tracker spent most of her life in my study, which had a carpeted cat tree, a window perch, and a variety of cat toys as well as her food and water bowls and her litter box, not to mention my computer, filing cabinet, books, and so forth. When Steve was home, we sometimes banished the dogs from our bedroom and let her sleep with us there. Steve was the only person she trusted. One of her few obvious pleasures was curling up next to him on his pillow. It was never clear to me if she actually enjoyed the freedom to explore the house that I sometimes provided when Rowdy and Kimi were outdoors or in their crates. In fact, she did little actual exploration and sometimes returned to my study on her own. Even so, I felt guilty about sentencing her to solitary confinement in my office and insisted on letting her out now and then, perhaps more for my sake than for hers.

Rowdy and Kimi's absence also offered the opportunity to let Sammy play with one of his beloved one-dog-only toys, which is to say, toys that dispensed food. I had phone calls to make, so instead of giving him the noisy Buster Cube, I packed pieces of cheddar into the three openings in a hard black rubber disc that was supposed to look like a spaceship. (The real name of the toy is a Kong X-treme Goodie Ship. No, I do not own stock in Kong or, for that matter, in Dyson or in the company that makes Dr. Noy's toys, either. I just wish I did.) Sammy watched eagerly as I jammed in the cheese; and when I had him sit in heel position, the tip of his tail flicked back and forth, his body almost vibrated, and his eyes gleamed. Still, when I told him what a good boy he was and presented him with the toy, he refrained from grabbing it and instead took it politely from my hand before dashing around in joy and then settling on the kitchen floor to chew out the bits of cheddar.

I then settled myself at the kitchen table and called one of my counterparts in Siberian husky rescue. As I expected, she had no news about Strike. She assured me that there had been posts about the lost Siberian on the sled dog lists and breed lists, and she promised to call me if she had any news.

Almost as soon as I hung up, the phone rang.

"Holly? Elise. Illinois rescue. I got your e-mail."

I thanked her for calling and said, "Actually, I have the dog now. The blue malamute. She was found running loose, so I know a little more about her. She's young, two or so, and I think she's a breeder dog. We can't find a spay scar, but we haven't done an ultrasound, so we're guessing. You know what that's like."

"Do I ever. The vet opens her up and finds she's already been spayed, and you end up paying the whole bill for a spay."

So why not do an ultrasound whenever there's a question? Ultrasound is expensive, and rescue groups need to control expenses. In some cases, there is no question: the shelter or the owner assures you that the dog has been spayed . . . and you get a surprise.

"We've had that happen, too." The *we* wasn't royal. Or maybe it was? I meant AM-RONE, Alaskan Malamute Rescue of New England.

"If she's intact, then we didn't place her," Elise said.

"Of course not." Every reputable rescue group spays or neuters all dogs before placing them unless the surgery would pose a health risk to the dog. For example, no sensible person subjects a fragile twelve-year-old male to neutering. Anyway, a firm spay-neuter policy is one hallmark of a good rescue group, and I didn't want Elise to feel insulted.

"But she doesn't sound like one of ours," Elise said. "The woman you asked about doesn't ring any bells, either, but I don't meet all of our adopters myself. I might see their applications, or I might talk to them on the phone. But —"

"I don't meet all of ours, either. If another volunteer works with an adopter, then maybe I'll meet the adopter at one of our events, but that's it."

"So, what'd you want to know about Grant?"

"The reason I'm interested in him is that he had blue in his lines. And not all that many people do." I explained the circumstances under which the photo had been found. "And the police still don't know who the murdered woman is. I thought that if I could find out who the dog is, then maybe that would help to identify the woman. I showed the photo to Phyllis Hamilton, and Grant was one of the breeders she mentioned as a possibility. Anyway, let me tell you what I know about him, which isn't much. Phyllis told me that he was a reputable breeder — or people thought he was a responsible breeder — and then his marriage went to pieces, and he got in some kind of financial trouble, and he disappeared. He got his dogs from Minnie Wilcox and Debbie Alonso."

"Poor Minnie," Elise said.

"Yes. I talked to her daughter."

"Her mind's gone. It's so sad. Debbie took responsibility for the dogs of Minnie's that Grant had. And her own. We got the rest."

"The ones Grant bred himself."

"Fourteen. Seven adults, seven puppies. His wife had left him, and he was living out there alone, and no one knew he was gone for maybe ten days. He just took off and left the dogs in their kennels, not that they'd been in great shape before. One of the males had an infected wound on his leg that hadn't been treated. It was a real mess getting that cleared up. And all of the dogs were starving, and not from being without food for just ten days. The kennels were filthy. What happened was that a neighbor noticed that Grant wasn't around and went to take a look. And found the dogs. Otherwise, they'd've all died. It's a good thing for

Grant that he took off. Everyone who saw that place and those dogs wanted to kill him."

"No wonder."

"And, Holly, these were such sweet dogs. They were real sweethearts. We placed all of them. They're loves."

"Any blue females?"

"One. One of the adults. She was five or so. But she's not the one you have. I see her all the time. I know the adopter."

"A puppy?"

"There was a blue male. That's it."

"Elise, when was this?"

"Two . . . two and half years ago, let's say. Yes. It was in April. What I heard was that Grant started getting in trouble the summer before that. You know about that?"

"No. Phyllis says that I might've met him at a National, but if I did, I don't remember. All I really remember is that you got a lot of his dogs."

"Well, the trouble was that his money, which he didn't have a lot of to begin with, was all going up his nose and into his veins. And his wife got sick of it, and she left him. I never met her. She didn't go to shows or anything. I heard she was a nice woman. Debbie Alonso knew her a little."

"You don't suppose . . . ?"

"That it's her? The one who was murdered?"

"Just a thought. How old is Grant?"

"Thirty-five? Forty, maybe."

"The murdered woman was probably too young to be his wife. She was in her early twenties. Still. I wonder how old Grant's wife is. Was? His ex-wife."

"You could ask Debbie."

"I will. Elise, do you have any idea what happened to Grant? Where he went?"

"To hell, I hope. That's where he belongs."

"In the meantime?"

"Someone told me he was in the Southwest. I heard that someone ran into him there. I don't care where he is as long as he doesn't have dogs."

"Do you remember who saw him?"

"Sorry. Someone told someone who . . . one of those things. This was maybe a year ago, anyway."

After that, we talked about rescue for a while. As soon as the call ended, I refilled Sammy's toy and called Debbie Alonso. The conversation was brief. Debbie had nothing good to say about Graham Grant. In fact, it sounded to me as if she was so furious at him that she could barely talk about him at all. His kennel name, I learned, had been Rhapsody. His wife was about his age, in her late thirties, Debbie thought. She certainly wasn't in her early twenties.

Feeling discouraged, I made two calls intended to cheer me up. The first was to Steve. Amazingly, I reached him. Just as amazingly, his cell phone didn't quit, so we had a long talk, during which I told him about everything except the murder and associated horrors. He'd be home on Saturday, and especially because we couldn't count on being able to reach each other by phone, I didn't want to worry him. Instead, I told him about the rally run-throughs I was going to the next evening, rally being a fun variety of obedience. Instead of performing a fixed set of exercises on the judge's orders, the dog and handler move through a course marked by signs. Each sign represents an exercise, sometimes a simple one like Halt, sometimes a more complicated one that involves, for example, heeling in a pattern around traffic cones. Anyway, a few months earlier, I'd had a flare-up of ring nerves, and although I was feeling almost ready to show again, I was still concentrating on lighthearted dog sports and avoiding competition obedience, which was formal, serious, and nerve-wracking, mainly because I made it that way. *Run-throughs,* I should add, are just what they sound like, opportunities to practice for trials under similar conditions but without actual competition and without scoring that counts. The run-throughs were taking place on the green of a suburban town. A pleasant evening spent playing with Rowdy was just what my healing nerves needed. Heeling nerves. Sorry. Punning is an affliction, presumably one with a neurological basis. Anyway, Leah and I were taking Rowdy and Kimi, and I was looking forward to time with Leah, too. I'd talked to her on the phone a couple of times, but I missed having her live with us.

My second cheer-myself-up call was to Gabrielle. I simply wanted to hear her voice, which, I was increasingly forced to recognize, always felt more maternal than my own mother's ever had. Force of habit, which is to say, the habit of addressing golden retrievers, had made Marissa sound like my handler and my breeder, as she was, of course, but my stepmother sounded like a mother and nothing more. Fortunately, it was Gabrielle and not Buck who answered, and she was filled with yet more excitement about drug enforcement and, in particular, about the DEA agent, Al, who was becoming a friend of hers. I was anything but surprised. Knowing my stepmother as I did,

I expected to find that Al would be joining us for Thanksgiving dinner at her house in Bar Harbor and that Gabrielle already had a list of suggestions about what Steve and I should give him for Christmas. I'd have bet anything that Gabrielle had invited him to use her guest cottage whenever he liked and to spend his next vacation there. So, I let Gabrielle's comforting warmth soothe me and paid little attention to the particulars about the latest complete stranger she was welcoming into our family. Out of the corner of my ear, I heard that the DEA confiscated all sorts of marvelous things. Raids yielded luxury vehicles and first-rate sound systems. Suspects were known as "subjects." Al sometimes went undercover. I knew that if he ever did anything iffy or odd or obnoxious, Gabrielle would tell me about it before adding in tones of shared affection, "But that's just Al. You know what he's like." If he did something truly egregious, she'd advise me to think of him as a difficult relative. She'd say it before I'd even met him.

But that's just Gabrielle. You know what she's like.

Yes, wonderful. I felt equally certain that my honorary cousin-to-be returned Gabrielle's affection. For obvious reasons, everyone loved her.

Although Gabrielle's chatter should have been an effective lullaby and although I had all three malamutes with me, I still felt uneasy at bedtime. To reassure myself, I checked the locks on all the doors and windows in the house, and I reminded myself that Kevin lived right next door. Then I loaded my Smith & Wesson and put it in the drawer of my nightstand. Why? Three reasons: Rowdy, Kimi, and Sammy. The woman who'd been stealing my name for herself had been stealing Kimi's identity for a malamute. I wouldn't have slept without the knowledge that I could protect my dogs.

CHAPTER 23

The other Holly Winter is a more private person than I am. Because of my volunteer work for malamute rescue, my name, address, and phone number are all over the World Wide Web, and when I call people, my name and number show up on caller ID. Why block my identity? When I call someone, the first words out my mouth when someone answers are going to be, "This is Holly Winter," so if caller ID has already transmitted the information, what do I care? And if someone sees my name on caller ID and decides not to answer? So what! In almost all circumstances, I'd rather get an answering machine or voice mail than force myself on someone who doesn't want to talk to me or who just feels like being left alone.

The other Holly Winter, however, has arranged never to have anyone's caller ID display her name and number. Our preferences in this regard reflect deep character differences that are, I believe, intimately tied to our radically divergent perspectives on Life Itself. Capitalized. What I mean by "Life Itself," capitalized, is . . . take a guess. Also take the matter of caller ID and Life Itself — or my very own Lives Themselves, so to speak, although not necessarily on the phone. Anyway, if the doggy equivalent of a phone company were to ask Lady, India, Rowdy, Kimi, and Sammy whether they wanted to hide or announce their identities when they were trying to reach people, the dogs would unanimously and vigorously veto the option of ID blocking. Once having agreed about the desirability of revealing their identities, they'd disagree about whether radical changes would be required in existing displays of caller ID. Lady, our timid pointer, would be content with the status quo: her name in plain, unassuming little letters. India, our proud shepherd, would push for the tasteful yet dignified: a gold-framed screen and elaborate Gothic script. The malamutes, however, would insist on neon signs the size of billboards that would flash their identities while simultaneously setting off simulated bursts of fireworks and deafening emissions of loud, brassy music. I can hear it now. Sammy would go for marching-band renditions of John Philip Sousa; Kimi would insist on references to glory, laud, honor, conquering heroes, and the trampling out of vineyards; and Rowdy, my Rowdy, would settle for nothing less than "Hail to the Chief."

Have I digressed? Anyway, on that same Monday evening, Holly Winter uses her caller-ID-blocked phone to dial a number in California. She gets an answering machine, hangs up, and tries another number, this one in Oregon. A human being answers but has nothing to say that interests Holly Winter. She tries several other numbers from her long list. Her quest is fruitless. So far. She will pursue her inquiries tomorrow.

CHAPTER 24

It may seem as if I never work. Not so! I spent Tuesday morning finishing a profile of a breed so obscure that I'd never heard of it until Bonnie, my editor at *Dog's Life,* gave me the assignment. In Bonnie's view, since the other dog magazines were publishing articles about popular breeds like the Labrador retriever and the cocker spaniel, we should go after readers by filling the niche left open by the competition. Yes, stupid idea. If your magazine has a photo of a Lab on the cover and an accompanying article inside, the issue is going to attract Lab devotees, of whom there are zillions. But why try to increase readership by attracting all six people in the country who have what even I, a born dog lover, felt to be the misfortune to spend their lives with the Breed Not to Be Named? In appearance, the BNTBN, as I shall tactfully call it, reminded me of the famous reference in

Sherlock Holmes to the giant rat of Sumatra: BNTBNs had snoutlike muzzles, small, beady eyes, and furtive expressions. The desired coat was short and brownish gray, the tail long and nearly hairless. Worse, instead of having originally served humankind by performing some appealing task such as herding sheep, pulling carts, guarding monasteries, or sitting in laps looking cute, this obscure breed had once specialized in doing a job so disgusting that I spent a half hour trying to come up with a suitable euphemism for it. So, you see? I don't exactly have a real job, but I certainly do work.

I finished the profile, e-mailed it to my editor, and went to Steve's clinic to check up on Miss Blue. The staff would reliably take excellent care of her, but I wanted to get to know her, in part to see whether her behavior had anything to tell me about her otherwise unknown owner and in part to help me think about the kind of home that would be best if she ended up as a rescue dog in need of an adopter. By two thirty, Miss Blue and I were in the park behind Loaves and Fishes, an area where the owners of dog-aggressive dogs sometimes cause problems by deciding that the therapy their dogs need is "socialization," meaning the chance to bound around off leash while perfecting their prowess in attacking other dogs. The advantage of the park behind Loaves and Fishes is that it's open, so you can at least watch for potential troublemakers instead of getting taken by surprise. Fortunately, the fields were uncrowded that afternoon, which was overcast and chilly, so I felt hopeful that I wouldn't need the aerosol boat horn and the citronella spray I was carrying in case I had to defend Miss Blue.

So far, she'd ignored a golden retriever running at his owner's side and a wonderfully assorted trio of terrier mixes all trotting together in front of an elderly woman who had the brisk gait of a teenager. In the middle of a field, I repeated my previous experiment of baiting Miss Blue and got the same result I'd had the previous day: she had no idea what I wanted. When I said, "Miss Blue, sit!" in my most thrilling dog-trainer tones — well, dogs are thrilled, anyway — she looked utterly delighted with herself as she slowly lowered her hindquarters to the grass and then immediately stood up again. My "Down!" did nothing except make her look vaguely puzzled. Translation: "But I wasn't up on anything! Why are you telling me to get down?" Obedience trainers use *down* exclusively to tell the dog to lie down. If the dog is countersurfing or, doG forbid, jumping on someone, we use *off* or some other command that doesn't confuse the dog. *Heel?* To her ears, the word came from a foreign language she didn't speak. So, as I expected, Miss Blue hadn't been trained for the show ring or the obedience ring.

But was she ever a great pet! When she made eye contact, as she did all the time, her eyes sparkled. Affectionate? She rubbed against me without shoving, and she had the delightful habit of raising her paw as if asking to hold hands. As she'd done the previous day, she dropped to the ground and rolled over to present her white tummy for rubbing. And someone had taught her to walk on leash without mistaking the activity for a weight-pull competition and without trying to dislocate the shoulder of the person at the other end of the leash. Feeling like a monster, I checked for hand shyness: I raised my hand and jerked it sharply toward her hindquarters and then toward her head. It goes without saying, I hope, that I hit nothing but air. Miss Blue didn't flinch. Steve's staff had seen no indication of what's called "resource guarding," in other words, growling and otherwise turning possessive in response to an effort to take away toys or treats. In a formal temperament test, the evaluator would've pushed Miss Blue hard to assess resource guarding. I'm not trained to do temperament tests, and I saw no reason to stress her. If she'd suddenly become my dog, I'd have played it safe by assuming that she'd guard her food and toys; I'd have taught her that an approaching hand meant food; and I'd have taught her to trade toys for treats. She wasn't going to become my dog, of course, and I'd been finding homes for homeless malamutes for too long to confuse my rescue dogs with my personal dogs. What enabled me to love the rescue dogs yet let them go was the joy they brought to the people who adopted them and the happiness the dogs felt in being home at last.

As Miss Blue and I began to move again, I glanced across the field and spotted a short woman in a bright yellow jacket who was walking a smooth fox terrier. *Smooth.* I should perhaps explain that in the parlance of purebred dogs, *smooth* describes the short coat of the Labrador retriever, the pointer, and lots of other breeds and mixes. The word is used mainly to differentiate between breeds or varieties characterized by distinctive coats. Lassie is a *rough* collie as opposed to a *smooth* collie. Nick and Nora's engaging Asta in the old *Thin Man* movies is a *wire* fox terrier rather than a *smooth* fox terrier like this one. So, my eye went first to the charming dog, who was, I noted with relief, on leash. After that, I noticed the woman's ever so slightly rolling, shuffling gait, which struck me as unusual in someone walking as quickly as she was. Belatedly, I recognized Mellie, who, of course, did dog walking.

As I was on the verge of calling out to her, Miss Blue beat me to it by bursting into peals of *woo-woo-woo, ah woo, ah woo-woo-woo-woo-woo.* Simultaneously, Mellie astonished me by shouting in that hoarse voice of hers while breaking into a run and barreling straight toward me — or, as it turned out, toward Miss Blue.

"Strike!" Mellie hollered. "Strike!"

Miss Blue's manners deserted her. She hit the end of her leash, and I went flying after her.

My only part in the reunion, as it obviously was, consisted of my leading Mellie's little client, the fox terrier, out of the way. In ecstasy, Miss Blue flung herself to the grass, rolled over, tucked in her paws, and eyed Mellie with the worshipful gaze that malamutes reserve for their objects of highest adoration, which is to say, anyone and everyone who has ever given them anything to eat. Mellie, for her part, got down on the damp ground, rubbed Miss Blue's underbelly, stood up, clapped her hands softly together, and, having lured Miss Blue to her feet, took the dog's big head gently in her hands and said, "I prayed to the Virgin every day for you. All the time, I lit candles. I was so . . ." Mellie choked up. Tears ran down her face.

I'm ashamed to admit that one of my first feelings was anger. I'd been looking for a Siberian husky. That's what I'd been told to look for, and I'd done exactly what I'd been asked to do. Why hadn't anyone . . . ? Then my anger turned inward. I should have known! All too clearly, I remembered Mellie's response when she'd first seen Rowdy: she'd said that Strike looked like Rowdy. But different, she'd added. Of course she'd looked different! She was smaller than Rowdy, a female, one with a blue coat and eyes lighter than Rowdy's near-black. So what? Over and over, I'd had my malamutes admired by people who said, "Beautiful huskies!" When Steve and I hiked with the dogs in Acadia National Park, we made a game of counting the number of times the malamutes were called huskies. But there'd been reasons for what now felt like my stupidity. In the American Kennel Club rankings, the Siberian husky was the twenty-fifth most popular breed, and the Alaskan malamute was the fifty-eighth; there were a lot more Siberians than there were malamutes. What's more, Siberians were the Houdinis of purebred dogdom, and when they escaped, they ran like crazy, fast and far away. In contrast, the typical malamute who got out of a fenced yard went straight to the nearest door to the house. Typical? What did that mean? Incredible though it seemed to me, there existed picky-eater malamutes and malamutes with almost no interest in food. As to escapism, malamutes did get loose and did get lost, and I'd heard of malamutes who not only tunneled under fences but who climbed chain link. Damn it! Strike had gone under Mellie's fence. She'd been seen heading for the back of Dr. Ho's house. I should have guessed.

I'd like to report that the moment I finally put one dog and one dog together to get one dog, everything else fell neatly into place. It did not. On the contrary, isolated fragments dropped in a jumble. Mellie's lost husky. The photo of the blue malamute found among the murder victim's belongings. The traces of dog hair also found there.

The "girl," as Mellie had said, who'd left Strike with her: the murdered woman, the woman who'd put my name, my address, and my phone number on . . . her own malamute. Or on someone else's? On this blue malamute, the same dog Mellie had lost, the same one I'd found.

"Go home with Mellie," I heard. "Now you get to come home with me."

Not a chance.

Had Mellie, too, made the connection between the murder victim and the woman who'd left Strike with her? Mellie did not make connections easily, I thought. Still, she must have made this one. She would simply have to talk to the police. Another fragment: Mellie's fear of the police. Was it really based on irrational anxiety about minor violations of dog-boarding regulations? Or was she justifiably worried about murder?

I tried to buy time. "Mellie," I said, "Strike can't go home with you right now. Strike looks healthy. And she feels healthy. But she needs to go to the vet. And stay there."

Mellie's face fell.

"It's not serious," I added. "Other dogs can't catch it. And she's going to be fine. But I have to take her back to the vet. The

211

good news is that she's safe. You can take down the flyers now, the posters I gave you." The terrier chose that opportune time to start bouncing impatiently at the end of his leash. "Besides, you have this dog to take care of. Strike is a big girl. You shouldn't try to walk both dogs at once."

"One at a time," Mellie said. She seemed to be repeating a rule. "Only one dog at a time. Unless they're both little."

"Exactly. And Strike isn't little. I'll take good care of her. I promise. She'll be fine. You don't need to worry about her anymore. She's safe now."

"I need to light candles." Mellie said. "You don't just ask. Father McArdle says so. You don't just ask. When you get what you want, you have to say thank you."

I nodded.

When I was driving Strike back to Steve's clinic, however, I realized that Mellie had applied the principle only to prayer. After all, I'd been the one who'd found the lost dog, hadn't I? But Mellie had been grateful to the Virgin and hadn't thanked me at all. Ridiculously, I felt shortchanged. But that's a dog-show type for you: competitive to the core. And if the competition happens to be the Mother of God? Especially then, you have to be a good sport.

CHAPTER 25

When I'd dropped Strike back at the clinic, I returned to my car and called Kevin Dennehy on my cell phone. He absolutely had to talk to Mellie, who lived right near the scene of the murder and who must have known the victim. As a cop, he needed to question her; and, as a Cambridge insider, he was in a far better position than I was to find out what should and should not be expected of her. Mellie, who had been taking care of Strike, must know something about the "girl" who'd left the malamute with her. Until now, I'd simply accepted Francie's statement that Mellie had special needs, and everything I'd observed about Mellie had confirmed Francie's original statements. Yes, Mellie took things literally. Yes, she seemed conscientious and sweet. She was fearful of authority and deeply religious. And she certainly loved dogs. But what did I really know about her? About her abilities, her strengths, her limitations? About what she would or would not do? Or what she might or might not have done. Someone at dog training had mentioned her parents: Father McArdle had promised Mellie's parents that he'd look out for her. Mrs. Dennehy had known them, Kevin had told me. Kevin himself would know something about Mellie's parents or could easily find people who'd known them well. Had Mellie's parents been people who'd have had a gun in the house?

After leaving Kevin an urgent message, I drove back to Loaves and Fishes, this time to run in and grab some food, as I should have done before returning Strike. I'd known that I was low on milk and that I'd need something to eat before leaving for the rally match. The weather was cool, so I could safely have left Strike in the car. The inefficiency was unlike me. I felt scattered. If I could just talk to Kevin, I'd have a sense of handing over responsibility. Then I'd spend the evening with Leah and the dogs. My love for my human and canine family would calm me, and the almost mystical fusion I'd experience in working with Rowdy would restore my focus. Throughout my life, whenever I have had the sense of losing myself, of not being myself or not being entirely who I am, I have become whole again by giving myself up to a dog I love. When I become half Rowdy and he becomes half me, when I am united with this dog I adore, that's when I am fully myself. My route to that union, and Rowdy's, too, I think, is teamwork. The obedience exercises, the familiar structure, the attention to tiny details, the concentration visible on Rowdy's face and audible in my voice, the hard-earned effortlessness with which we move as one, all of it becomes my most powerful version of prayer and my most reliable source of renewed faith and redemption.

So, I intended to breeze through Loaves and Fishes. Besides milk, I needed roast beef, some for the sandwich I'd have instead of a real dinner, some for Rowdy's what-a-good-boy treat after the rally event. Loaves and Fishes, I should mention, is not some little gourmet shop but a big, crowded supermarket with departments for fish, meat, and cheese, its own bakery, a deli, and, of course, the sushi bar where Dr. Ho was reputed to have picked up his, ahem, take-out. It was at the deli counter, near the innocent yet, to my mind, infamous sushi bar that I encountered the other Holly Winter. By "encountered," I do not mean that I sought her out. On the contrary, if I hadn't been waiting for the pound of sliced roast beef that I'd asked for, I'd have avoided her by walking away. It was she who accosted me. In fact, I thought for a second that she was going to ram me with her cart, but she brought it to halt and said, "Fancy seeing you here."

Ridiculous! Loaves and Fishes is a place where you see everyone. I might as well have been in front of the Coop in Harvard Square. Or, now that I think of it, on the sidewalk on Mass. Ave. in front of Mr. Bartley's Burger Cottage. But what was her implication? That I belonged in a junk-food warehouse? Or that there was something suspect about my being where she was?

"Fancy seeing *you* here, too," I said.

"Strange coincidence."

"The world is full of coincidences," I said, without adding anything about my canine-cosmological belief that the apparent meaninglessness of any co-occurrence results from a failure to see what the co-occurring elements actually have in common, namely, dogs. But did I really want to argue with a statistician about probability or correlation? I wouldn't have minded. My religious beliefs, however, are private. I didn't feel like sharing them with an infidel.

"You just so happen to be here, to have

my name, and to have found the body of a woman who stole my identity." Holly Winter, the other one, spoke with the distinctive air of believing herself to possess secret knowledge.

I was determined not to get in anything even remotely like a shouting match. Almost whispering, I said, "You haven't been harmed, and I'm tired of your insinuations. I did not steal or try to steal your name or your identity. It happens to be my name, too," I said. "It's the one I was born with."

As an aside, let me issue a plea: if you give birth to a girl whose last name is going to be Winter, please do not call her Holly. My parents had an excuse: their previous experience in bestowing appellations had consisted exclusively of selecting registered names and call names for golden retrievers.

"Were you?" I asked Holly Winter. "Born with it?" The effort to keep my voice low was beginning to wear me down.

"You make it sound like a genetic disease," she said.

The comeback made me uncomfortable, sounding as it did like exactly the kind of thing I might have said myself. Glancing at the top of the glass deli counter, I saw that my package of roast beef was ready. The conversation, if you could call it that, was going nowhere. I picked up my package and walked away.

CHAPTER 26

Holly Winter dials a number in Arizona and is almost surprised to have someone answer, a man with a rough voice who coughs loudly. Representing herself as an attorney calling from a law firm in Boston, she states, without giving her name or the firm's name, that she is trying to trace the heir to a substantial amount of money. Had I been making such a call, I'd have invented names for myself and for the fictitious law firm: "Attorney Charlotte Dickens here," I might have said. "With Black and Lodge." Or in rebellion against the media-free movement, I might have presented myself as Barbie Thomas of Toynbee and Trainer. But I'm not the one making the call. She is. On the one hand, she displays no imagination. On the other hand, she knows when to keep her mouth shut. In fact, she listens.

Eventually, she says, "Maine?" She realizes that her tone makes it sound as if she has never before heard of the state of Maine or as if Maine were some exotic place on a distant continent: "Belarus?"

Having jotted a number down on a scrap of paper, she ends the conversation and immediately dials a number that begins with an area code I dial all the time: 207. Maine. A mechanical voice informs her that she has reached the number she just dialed. She hangs up.

She then turns to Google.

Google. The World Wide Web. Fondness for it. We have more in common, she and I, than I like to admit.

She first does exactly what I'd do — she enters the 207 number — but gets no results. Her next try — Maine meth OR methamphetamine — yields many results, in fact, a plethora. She opens a few Web pages and scans for information. Like me, she is a fast reader, in part because she skims material that she already knows. For instance, she doesn't need to read every word about Maine's long border with Canada. She changes her search: dogs meth OR methamphetamine. Here, I cannot refrain from pointing out that using the operator OR between synonyms is unnecessary and, to my eye, clumsy. I'd use a tilde: dogs ~meth. But no one is looking over her shoulder. Specifically, I'm not. In other words, we are not competing. Still, what she discovers is something I could have told her, namely, that drug dealers have been known to smuggle their goods through U.S. Customs in the digestive tracts of dogs. And, as is incidental to her search and to my story, in the innards of human beings, too.

She picks up her phone and calls the police.

CHAPTER 27

When I got home, another fragment fell in place. *Strike.* Mellie had been told that the dog's name was Strike. She'd also been told, as far as I could tell, that Strike was a husky and that she had been spayed. If I wanted my dogs to respond to names other than their real ones, I'd pick names that sounded at least somewhat similar: India would pose a problem, as would Rowdy, but Lady could become Baby, Kimi could be Ginny, Sammy could be Ranny. Miss Blue. Strike. Streak. Indeed, Blue Streak. Grant's kennel name? Rhapsody. Her registered name? Rhapsody's Blue Streak. I'd have put money on it. I'd have lost. I took a quick look at the Alaskan Malamute Registry Pedigree Program and practically hit myself over the head. I should've known! I, who considered myself an expert on canine nomenclature, had failed to predict the perfectly predictable, which was that in registering his dogs, his *malamutes,* the world-class *woo-woo-woo-*ers of the dog world, he'd substituted — you guessed, huh? — *woo* for *blue.* The dogs he'd bought from Minnie Wilcox and Debbie Alonso bore their kennel names, Snosquall and Crevasse: Snosquall Rhapsody in Woo and Crevasse Midnight Woo, as I'd have discovered if I'd searched for owners named Grant instead of for dogs with blue names. How like me to have focused on dogs rather than on people! How stupid! Anyway, the dogs of his own breeding included Rhapsody's Sky Woo and Rhapsody's Rhythm N Woos. Rhapsody's Woo Streak wasn't in the database, which had information on dogs that had been bred and had thus had their names published in studbooks, and dogs with names published elsewhere. Lots of malamutes weren't in the database. The absence meant nothing. Streak was Rhapsody's Woo Streak. I finally knew who she was.

She'd been bred by Graham Grant. And owned by . . . ? She'd been tagged with my name. At the risk of immodestly expanding on a matter I've already touched on, I have to say that in the world of purebred dogs and especially in the world of malamutes, I am someone. I write for *Dog's Life.* My articles have appeared there and in other dog magazines. I wrote the text for a book of photographs of the legendary old Morris and Essex dog shows, I'm the author of a book called *101 Ways to Cook Liver* that's mainly about training with food, and Steve and I were the coauthors of a soon-to-be-published dog-diet book called *No More Fat Dogs.* I showed my dogs, I posted to all of the e-mail lists about malamutes, I did malamute rescue, and in short, I made my presence known. Anyone with malamutes could have known who I was. Graham Grant and I had evidently met at an Alaskan Malamute National Speciality. I didn't remember him, but even if he'd forgotten meeting me there, he simply had to know my name. When he'd gotten himself in trouble and disappeared, he'd abandoned his dogs. All of his dogs? So it was assumed. It seemed possible that he'd taken one with him, a puppy, an especially promising puppy: Rhapsody's Woo Streak. Had he sold her to someone? Had someone stolen her from him? The murder victim, the unidentified woman, had been stealing identities; she'd been an identity thief. Had she been a dog thief, too? Exactly what did Mellie know about her? And maybe about her murder? And what did Kevin know about Mellie herself? What could he find out?

With no success, I again tried to reach Kevin at every number I had. The last number was the one he shared with his mother. A Seventh-Day Adventist, Mrs. Dennehy refused to have meat or alcohol in the house, and she'd always felt a little resentful about my willingness to make room in my refrigerator for Kevin's hamburger and beer. Also, before Kevin got involved with Jennifer Pasquarelli and before I married Steve, Mrs. Dennehy had harbored the suspicion that her son and I were also sharing space that was more hot than cold. Still, to her credit, she'd always been polite and even pleasant to me, in fact, more pleasant than she was to Jennifer, whom she simply couldn't stand.

"Mrs. Dennehy? Holly. I'm trying to reach Kevin," I said, "but I haven't had any luck."

"That Jennifer! That's where he is. Pouring oil on troubled waters. She was sent to this training course, and what did she go and do? Sent there to learn to be nice to people, and could she manage that for as much as a week? The little miss could not. Lost that temper of hers, that's what she did. Stamped her little feet and marched out and got in her car and drove home. And that's where my Kevin is now. In Attleboro, of all places, trying to help her out. Pearls before swine!"

It was the most uncharitable remark I'd ever heard Mrs. Dennehy make. In fact, so far as I could recall, it was the only one.

"He isn't answering his cell phone," I said. "And I don't have Jennifer's number."

"I don't have it. And don't want it."

"I'm very sorry to hear that there's trouble," I said. "I won't bother you anymore. Just, uh, if you talk to Kevin, could you tell him to call me? I have to go out soon. I should be home at nine or so."

"You're a good girl," she said, as if making an implicit comparison. "Kind to animals."

When we'd said good-bye, it occurred to me that for all of Jennifer's difficulties in getting along with people, especially the residents of Newton whom she was supposed to protect, she'd never shown any animosity to animals. She was a tiger about the leash law and the pooper-scooper law, but she correctly blamed violations on dog owners rather than on dogs, and, in any case, behavior even bordering on unkindness to animals would've driven Kevin off long ago. How he tolerated her impossible attitude toward people was, however, beyond me. If he married Jennifer, he'd spend the rest of his life doing what I suspected he was doing now, namely, to use his mother's phrase, pouring oil on troubled waters. At a guess, he was talking sense into Jennifer and also trying to talk the people in charge of the training course into giving Jennifer another chance. He might even succeed. While I wouldn't go quite so far as to call Jennifer a swine, Kevin truly was a pearl among men.

Mindful of the time, I tried to work out a plan. There was no reason to wait for Kevin to question Mellie. In fact, she might speak more freely to me than she would to anyone in authority, even Kevin, and I could pass along whatever she told me. The run-throughs started at six thirty. I'd need to leave Cambridge by about five forty-five. It was now four thirty. The dogs wouldn't mind eating early, and I could have a quick sandwich, put Rowdy and Kimi in the van, pay a visit to Mellie, get Leah, and arrive at the event more or less on time. I placed a quick call to Mellie to ask whether I could stop in. She said yes. I put the plan into operation: feed dogs; feed self; change clothes, fresh, not fancy; give Rowdy and Kimi a minute in yard; crate them in van; give Sammy five minutes in yard; crate him in kitchen; go!

CHAPTER 28

As I'd done the first time I'd visited Mellie, I avoided the hassle of parallel-parking the van on the narrow, car-lined street by pulling into her driveway. For once, I chose not to take the dogs with me to a place I knew they'd be welcome. At Mellie's, Rowdy, Kimi, or both would be all too welcome. She'd fuss over them, and she'd be so distracted that I'd never persuade her to tell me anything about the woman who'd entrusted her with Strike. Streak. Rhapsody's Woo Streak? With the blue malamute.

The small areas of grass on either side of the steps to Mellie's porch were freshly mown, and a pot of yellow mums sat next to her front door. Was it Mellie herself, I wondered, who tended the grass and who had bought the fall flowers? How much could she and had she done for herself? Could she possibly have had anything to do with . . . ? I rang the bell, and when she opened the door, I felt like a fool for suspecting someone who looked as thoroughly harmless as Mellie did. Her round face was guileless, and as she invited me in, I sensed nothing but warmth and genuineness. As usual, she wore bright colors: a green sweatshirt and matching pants. As on my previous visit, I was struck by the colorful pillows and the other cheerful objects that brightened what would otherwise have been the overwhelmingly brown and depressing decor of the living room. I wondered whether Mellie's parents had chosen the religious paintings or whether Mellie herself had selected *The Last Supper* and the *Madonna and Child.* Although neither picture was outright gloomy, *The Last Supper* was, of course, the last one, and both the Madonna and the infant Jesus looked pensive and slightly jaundiced. I had a hunch that on her own, Mellie would have picked biblical images that included animals and that expressed themes of happiness and hope: Christ with a symbolic flock of sheep, the Magi at the stable.

"You want coffee?" Mellie asked. I was getting used to the hoarseness of her voice and to her habit of speaking a little more loudly than necessary.

"No, thanks. I'm on my way somewhere,

so I can't stay long."

"You want to sit down?"

I accepted the offer and took a seat on one of the brown chairs. Mellie sat on the couch facing me.

"I'm scared," she said.

"About Strike? She's fine. And she's going to be all healthy very soon. But her vet needs help. Her vet needs to know what shots she's had."

"Up-to-date on all shots." It was one of the times when Mellie spoke as if she were repeating a phrase she'd memorized.

"Do you have her rabies certificate?"

Mellie's face went blank.

"Mellie, you know what a rabies certificate is. It's a piece of paper proving that a dog has had a rabies shot, a shot that stops the dog from getting sick with rabies."

Mellie remained silent, but her round face became pinched.

"And other vet records? About other shots?"

Still no luck.

I went on. "Mellie, shots hurt."

Mellie almost shouted in agreement: "I hate shots!"

"I do, too," I said truthfully. "And so do dogs." Some more than others. Rowdy had never shown any sign of minding them at

230

all. I didn't say so. "We don't want Strike to have to have shots she doesn't need, do we?"

Mellie said nothing.

"And heartworm medicine. You know what that is."

"The first day of January, February, March, all of them."

"Exactly. So that the dog doesn't get sick from heartworm." I paused. "And September first. Strike. Did you give Strike her medicine on September first?"

Mellie laughed. "Of course!"

So, Streak had been with Mellie then. "And the girl who left her with you gave you the medicine for Strike."

All the bright good humor left Mellie's face. She locked her jaw.

"And Strike might like to have her own blanket. Or toys."

"Don't tell." Mellie again seemed to be echoing someone else's words.

I took a guess. "You promised. You made a promise not to tell."

Mellie burst into tears. I felt like a monster. "Mellie, I'm sorry. I didn't mean to make you cry. You don't need to cry. I'm so sorry." I moved to the couch beside her and took her hand. "Look, I have an idea. You're having a hard time figuring out what to do.

I think you're not sure what the right thing is."

She nodded.

"Father McArdle is a friend of yours, isn't he?"

Her face brightened. "You know Father McArdle?"

"I know who he is," I said. "I live right near Saint Peter's Parish. I think you should talk to Father McArdle. And ask his advice. Ask him about the right thing to do. Okay?"

"Yeah."

"Sometimes it's hard to know the right thing. And all of us need help deciding. And when we do, we ask other people. Can you call Father McArdle? Do you have his phone number? Do you ever call him?"

"And he calls me, too." She sounded wonderfully proud. "He says, 'Mellie, how are you?' And he asks what I'm doing."

"Well, this time, you need to call him. You can ask how he is and what he's doing, and then you can tell him about Strike and about promises. And you can ask him what to do. Okay?"

"Yeah."

"Promise?"

She didn't make the connection. Solemnly, she said, "I promise."

I knew she'd make the call. After all, she certainly did keep promises.

CHAPTER 29

What I knew about Roman Catholicism was almost nothing. In particular, I knew almost nothing about confession except what everyone learns from movies and TV shows, for example, that priests were forbidden to reveal anything they'd learned during confession. What had Mellie told her priest about Strike and about the woman who'd left Strike with her? What, if anything, had she said to him about the murder? Mellie and her priest spoke on the phone and probably in person. If she'd told him anything important about the murder victim or the murder, had she done so in an informal conversation? Or during confession? In any case, I somehow trusted Father McArdle to advise Mellie to talk to the police, if not to me, and to be fully truthful in spite of whatever promise of secrecy she'd made about Strike. From what I'd heard, he sounded like a good man. After all, according to Mellie, he had assured her that her Boston terrier, Lily, had gone to heaven. That assurance continued to comfort her.

I thought of the priest as I passed Saint Peter's Parish at nine or nine fifteen that evening. I'd dropped Leah off after the run-throughs and was looking forward to getting home. At the start of the evening, as we'd headed out of Cambridge, I'd thought about presenting the entire story to Leah, but I'd decided that she'd have nothing useful to say about it. On the contrary, I was sure that she'd suggest pressing Mellie far more forcefully than I wanted to do. Not that Leah was a mean or inconsiderate person. She was kind, but she'd never met Mellie and wouldn't understand why I was unwilling to try to shake the truth out of her. Speaking of truth, I have to confess that I had a selfish reason for avoiding the subject of Mellie, Streak, and the murder: I wanted a few hours of respite and escape, and once Leah gets started on something, she just won't let it go. So, I got what I wanted. Leah was bubbling with news of her friends and her courses, and I enjoyed listening to her and sharing her happiness. In return, I told Leah about Gabrielle's new friendship with the DEA agent whom she met because someone had been growing marijuana on land she owned, the same DEA agent who was probably going to turn up at Thanksgiving dinner and become our honorary cousin.

At the rally event, I ran into a lot of people I knew, and Rowdy did exceptionally well, even on an advanced exercise called the Offset Figure 8 that required him to refrain from devouring the contents of two bowls of little dog cookies. According to the rules for rally novice and advanced, the handler is allowed to communicate with the dog during exercises by talking, patting her leg, clapping her hands, and otherwise providing encouragement, but I'm far from sure that the people who wrote the rules understood that a malamute handler determined to keep her dog's attention away from food has to blast the dog with every allowed form of encouragement all at once. Talking is easy: "Good boy, Rowdy! That's it! Excellent! This way! Perfect!" Fine. But just try slapping your thigh while simultaneously clapping your hands. I mean, it can't be done, can it? You'd need three hands. Well, as an alternative, what you'd really need is liver, beef, or chicken, all three of which I used in quantity. Food isn't allowed during actual trials, but this was a run-through, and I make no apologies. I got the behavior

I wanted. That was my goal. I achieved it. And Rowdy and I both had fun. Kimi, I might add, got the little dog cookies in the bowls. She had fun, too.

I spent the drive back to Cambridge persuading Leah to stop blaming herself.

"It was just a little setback," I said.

"She'll remember it forever. I haven't been working with her. I knew it was too advanced."

"Leah, rally is supposed to be fun. So a malamute stole food. That's news to you?"

"Rowdy didn't."

"He isn't crazy about those dry cookies."

"I should've used treats the way you did."

"Next time you will, okay? For now, just let it go. Kimi had a happy experience with rally. Focus on that."

"You and your positive methods! I half wish you were still using choke collars."

"You do not!"

"I do. At least you didn't use them on me."

So, I had a good time, in fact, such a good time that it wasn't until I was driving up Concord Avenue past Saint Peter's that I again began to worry and to wonder about Mellie, and to hope that Kevin had finally freed himself from the impossible task of rescuing Jennifer from her social-skills-training fiasco. As I turned left onto Huron

Avenue, I found myself missing Steve and wishing that he, Leah, and Rita hadn't all departed at the same time. I should explain that although my house faces Concord Avenue, the driveway is on Appleton Street, which is one-way. From the Square, I take Concord to Huron, turn left, and then go right on Appleton, as I did that night. When I pulled the van into the driveway, I saw nothing out of the ordinary. The exterior of our house is exceptionally well illuminated. There are so many lights that we'd be guilty of polluting the environment if we routinely used all of them. Fortunately, they have separate switches, so we limit ourselves to turning on the lights we need when we need them. Because I knew I'd be coming home after dark, I'd turned on some lights on the back of the house, enough for me to see that there was no one around. Next door, Kevin's car wasn't in his usual spot in the driveway, but the windows in the Dennehys' living room showed the glow of the television. Mrs. Dennehy was waiting up for her son. When I opened the door of the van, I heard the muffled ring of the phone in my kitchen. The machine was set to pick up after the phone had rung eight times. Had it just started to ring? Was Kevin trying to call me? Or Steve? Maybe Steve had reached a place where his cell phone worked. Maybe he'd tried to call me on mine. It was in my purse, but I'd turned it off. Damn! I should've remembered to turn it on and check for messages before starting back home.

With my key ring still in my hand, I quickly locked the van, ran the few feet to the back steps, and sprinted up to the door. The dogs would be fine in the locked van; a back window was open. My purse, too, was in the van, as were empty spring-water bottles, a little cooler that I'd used for fresh dog treats, and other odds and ends that I'd carry into the house after I took the phone call. I put the key in the lock and opened the outer back door, which leads to a small hallway, little more than a landing, with a door to the cellar and with stairs that run up to the second floor and to Rita's third-floor apartment. Straight ahead is the door to our kitchen. I'd unlocked my outer back door thousands of times, of course. The phone was still ringing, and I was in such a hurry to answer it that I can't even remember the automatic act of unlocking the outer door and pushing it inward. When I opened the door, it never occurred to me that in my rush to leave the house, I'd failed to make sure that the outer door was locked. I can recall no sense whatever of the presence of another person in that small space.

The first thing I remember is what the man said: "You have some things that belong to me. I want them back."

He was standing behind me. For a moment, it seemed as if he had materialized out of nowhere; caught off guard, I was too startled and frightened to realize that he'd already been in the hallway when I'd entered. It seemed to me that I was caught in a recurring nightmare: I enter my own house to find a strange man there who says that I have something of his and who wants me to hand it over. Since I have no idea what he means, I can't just get rid of him by giving him what he wants. This second version of the scene was, however, different from the first. Adam's Harley had been parked in my driveway. Leah had let him in. "You have something for me," he'd said. Adam hadn't implied that the something belonged to him; he'd seemed to expect me to pass the unknown something along to him rather than to give it back. But the big difference, the terrifying difference, was that Adam hadn't tried to scare me. "Hope I didn't startle you," he'd said. Furthermore, there'd been nothing threatening about his manner; he'd been perfectly pleasant. In comparison with the man in the hallway, Adam now seemed like the ideal guest. Why the hell had I dashed for the phone? Cell phones work both ways. If Steve could call me, I could call him back. Damn it all! Why had I left my big dogs in the van?

"You have the wrong person," I said. "You have me confused with someone else." The tactic had worked with Adam. It was worth trying again this time.

"Holly Winter," he said. His voice was unfamiliar. I was still facing the kitchen door, and he was still in back of me. I hadn't had so much as a glimpse of him.

"This happens all the time," I said. "There's another Holly Winter in Cambridge. People get us confused." My voice was steady. Truly, it was.

"You have malamutes. You do rescue. You write for *Dog's Life*. Now, open that door."

The phone had stopped ringing. The caller had hung up without waiting to hear the recorded message. The silence made me feel entirely cut off.

I said, "I prefer not to."

"We can do this nice. Or not. Now open the door and give me my stuff." A sharp, pointed object pressed into my back. "Including my bitch," he said. The dog person's word, *bitch*. That's when I began to suspect who he was.

I opened the door and flipped on the light. In his wire crate, Sammy rose to his feet and shook himself all over. I felt overwhelmed with love for him and overwhelmed with regret that it was puppy-brained Sammy in that crate instead of Rowdy. If Rowdy had been there? He'd immediately have sensed the threat and taken action, and the crate wouldn't have stopped him. In comparison with our expensive Central Metal crates, this wire one was flimsy. I'd bought it as a travel crate because I'd hated lugging the heavy ones. We used it in the kitchen because it was easy to fold and put away, and also because Sammy liked it. If Rowdy had wanted to get out of it, he'd have destroyed it in seconds.

The man slammed the door shut. "Beautiful puppy," he said. *Puppy.* Only a real dog person would've realized how young Sammy was. "Great bone. Nice Kotzebue head."

Correct. Three strains — Kotzebue, M'Loot, and Irwin-Hinman — contributed to today's Alaskan malamutes. The Kotzebue dogs were the original malamutes bred by Milton and Eva B. ("Short") Seeley at the Chinook Kennels in Wonalancet, New Hampshire. Short Seeley had strong opinions about malamute head type. Among other things, she bred for small ears and a soft expression that comes, in part, from dark, almond-shaped eyes set at just the right angle. Sammy had Rowdy's beautiful Kotzebue head. When this man looked at Sammy, he knew what he was seeing.

Graham Grant.

I turned and finally got a look at him. Yes, somewhere, sometime I had seen him, presumably at the National Speciality where Phyllis Hamilton had said I'd met him. On that occasion, he must've looked better than he did now. How he looked now was like all hell after a bad accident. Elise had told me that Graham Grant was thirty-five or forty, as he appeared to be. He was maybe five-ten, with a wide build and massive shoulders, but his grubby brown-plaid flannel shirt and stained jeans hung loose, and his face was gaunt. The shagginess of his straight brown hair suggested the need for a barber rather than the pursuit of trendiness, and around his hazel eyes was a raccoon mask that was fading from black to green and brown. He needed a bath, a shave, a haircut, a change of clothes, and a month of three squares a day. More important, he needed to get rid of the hunting knife he held in his right hand.

"Thank you," I said. "I'm biased, of

course. But all he needs to finish is one major."

"My stuff."

"I have no idea what you mean. If I did, I'd give it to you. Search the house if you want. I have no idea what you're talking about."

"Including my blue bitch."

"I don't know what to tell you except what I've already said. You're welcome to look. If you don't believe me, look for yourself."

I expected him to put the knife to my throat or maybe to slap or punch me. What he did was far worse. He deftly undid the latch to Sammy's crate, waited for Sammy to emerge, wrapped his left hand around Sammy's collar, and put the knife to Sammy's throat. "My stuff," Grant said coolly. "Now."

Chapter 30

I could think of nothing except the Smith & Wesson sitting uselessly in the drawer of my nightstand in our bedroom on the second floor of the house. The distance between the kitchen and that nightstand seemed like a thousand miles. At the same time, I could almost feel the weight of the revolver in my hand. My right index finger twitched. I am an excellent shot. Exercising the gift, however, requires a weapon.

Before I could respond to Grant's repeated demand, a demand I'd have met if I'd been able, Grant suddenly did something peculiar. Background: I'd left the house in a hurry. In spite of my haste, I'd put the plate I'd used for my sandwich in the dishwasher, where I'd also put the dog bowls. Under the table, however, was one object I'd overlooked and thus failed to tidy up: Sammy's Pink Piggy, in one of his three manifestations. To my astonishment, Grant pointed to it and said, "Cut the bullshit. Pick it up."

Pink Piggy? For a second, fear stole my power of rational thought. Could it possibly be true that Graham Grant had invaded my house and was holding a knife to Sammy's throat because I'd left a dog toy on the floor? Because I hadn't finished the housework?

In what felt like a moment of temporary insanity, I obeyed the order. "It's nothing," I said. "But you can have it if you want."

Sammy's gleaming eyes were on Pink Piggy. His full white tail was waving over his back. I took care not to squeeze the toy; if Sammy heard the squeaker, he'd be likely to leap for Pink Piggy, with consequences I didn't want to risk.

I said, "It's nothing but an old toy. Look at it. You can see how worn it is. It's a Dr. Noy's toy. That's all it is."

"Open it."

"If I do, my dog is going to go for it."

Grant tightened his grip on Sammy's collar. I ripped the Velcro apart, extracted the pouch, opened it, removed the squeaker, and put all the parts of the toy on the kitchen table.

"There," I said.

"The rest of them," Grant ordered.

"There are two more somewhere. Just like this one. Old toys. With new squeakers."

"Cut the bullshit!"

"I have no idea what you mean. If I did, I'd give you whatever you want."

"It was in the paper. The body was found by Holly Winter. You. You were the first person there."

"I have already told you that there's another Holly Winter. She lives in Cambridge. I cannot help it that we have the same name." As I spoke, I frantically tried to think of a plan. If I could distract him, then . . . ? Then I could somehow knock the phone off the hook? If Sammy broke away, then . . . ? Then I could scream and hope that someone heard me? Mrs. Dennehy? Another neighbor? Kevin, returning home, getting out of his car, hearing me, and coming to my rescue, mine and Sammy's? Or if Sammy freed himself and ran upstairs, I could bolt after him, race to the nightstand, and get my hands on my Smith & Wesson?

"This is getting real old," he said.

"There *is* another Holly Winter. That's true. And she has to be the one you're looking for. I'm the one who found the body, but that's all I did." If Sammy got away? He could end up with knife wounds. Fatal wounds. Or deadly bullets in his perfect body. There was no reason to believe that the knife was Grant's only weapon. "I looked in through the glass door of a house," I said. "I called the police. End of story."

"Beautiful puppy you got here. Too bad you don't give a damn about him."

Sammy knew that something was wrong. The sight of Pink Piggy had misled him into imagining that we were playing some kind of new game, one he didn't understand, but one that might turn out to be fun. Now, he was catching on.

"Okay. Look, I'm just trying to stay out of whatever mess this is. Here's what happened. A guy showed up here. Adam, his name was. And I gave him what I found. All of it. He had a Harley. A new-looking Harley. Top of the line. With a Maine plate. He was a big, tall guy with curly black hair. Does any of that ring any bells with you? Because that's who has your stuff. Adam. And that's all I know about him. I should've said so to begin with, but he was a big, scary biker. He scared me. All I want is to stay out of this."

I wished that I were half as good at reading human beings as I am at reading dogs. Canine communication was my first language: facial expressions, body postures, vocalizations, all of it. Graham Grant was showing a response of some kind to what I'd said, but I couldn't decipher exactly what he was making of my words. His eyes, in particular, were so flat and dead that they were hard to read. When I was describing Adam and the Harley, I thought that recognition flashed briefly across Grant's face, but I just couldn't be sure.

"This guy look like he came out of the Bible?" Grant asked. "One of those movies about the Bible?"

"Yes! That's exactly what he looks like. Moses. He reminded me of Moses."

"Son of a bitch," Grant said.

The conviction in his voice sent waves of relief surging through me. My knees felt so weak that I sank into one of the kitchen chairs.

That's when the phone rang. And wrecked everything.

"Don't answer it," Grant said.

I waited in silence as the phone rang again and again. Eight times? Yes, eight rings that felt like a hundred. Finally, I heard my own voice say, "You have reached Holly Winter, Dr. Steve Delaney, and Alaskan Malamute Rescue. Please leave a message." The machine emitted its annoying tone. I heard the caller breathe loudly. "This is Mellie O'Leary." She spoke with the anxiety and formality of someone unused to leaving recorded messages. "Father McArdle says I have to give you Strike's toys." She paused. "He says that not telling is lying, too." Again she paused. "And it's a sin," she finished.

Grant laughed. "You hear that? It's a sin, you lying bitch. We're taking your car." He grabbed a short leash from the rack on the back of the kitchen door. "Put this on your puppy." I obeyed. Up close to Grant, I felt sickened by the stench of filth. "You first."

Where were my keys? For a panicked second, I couldn't remember. Then I spotted them on a counter, picked them up, and opened the door to the little back hallway. The murdered woman had, in fact, left some of Streak's possessions with Mellie. Streak's? The woman's own possessions? Possessions that belonged to Graham Grant. Or so he thought. Dog toys. Toys like Pink Piggy used as Velcro-fastened hiding places for who knew what. I, at least, didn't care. All I wanted was to get Mellie to give those toys to Grant. And after that? After that, would he go away and leave us alone? Or would he . . . damn it! I'd almost forgotten. He wanted his blue bitch. Streak was at Steve's clinic. Panic rose again. I'd worry about Streak later, about Grant's next demand, about whatever Grant might do to us once he had whatever he wanted.

Behind me, I heard Sammy's tags jingle. Grant followed me through the little hallway, out the door, and down the stairs. A glance showed me that Kevin still wasn't home; his spot in the Dennehys' driveway was still empty. I thought about warning Grant that I had two dogs in the van, but why tell him that he could have three canine hostages instead of one? But if Rowdy or Kimi startled him, would he overreact? I thought not; it wouldn't come as a surprise to Grant that I was surrounded by dogs. And who knew? Rowdy or Kimi might somehow prove useful, especially if Grant failed to realize that they were in the van. They'd had a busy evening, and they were used to riding contentedly in their crates. For once, I was glad that Steve's rattletrap actually rattled. When it was moving, it would help to camouflage any low sounds that Rowdy and Kimi might make, and the jingle of their tags might be mistaken for the jingle of Sammy's.

"You're driving," Grant said. "Get in. And don't forget what's right here at your puppy's throat."

The second I was in the driver's seat, I started the noisy engine, and by the time Grant had opened the passenger door, I had the fan going at full clatter and had made sure that my purse was on the floor right next to me. There was no time to unzip my purse and get my cell phone, but the proximity of the phone increased my confidence, as did the knowledge that Rowdy was in the crate just behind my seat; and Kimi, in the crate beyond Rowdy's. To prevent Grant's attention from wandering to the crated dogs, I turned on the radio, changed the station from NPR to old rock, and started talking. "Mellie O'Leary lives near here. We'll be there in five or ten minutes."

Grant positioned Sammy between the front seats, settled himself in the passenger seat, and slammed the door. On the radio, Roy Orbison sang "Crying." Damn it! I hoped that the dogs wouldn't be inspired to accompany Orbison by howling along.

"Incredible," I said over the soaring of that astonishing voice and the static of the radio. "Amazing range. You know, Bruce Springsteen said that he wished he could write like Bob Dylan and sing like Roy Orbison."

Backing the van out into Appleton Street is always a challenge. The street is narrow to begin with, and both sides are always lined with parked cars. I tried to focus my attention on maneuvering the van while letting the chatter take care of itself.

"There was a TV special on a while ago about Roy Orbison," I blathered. "With Bruce Springsteen and lots of other people. Bonnie Raitt. And Roy Orbison himself. We're going to take Concord Avenue, this street, to the Fresh Pond rotary and then get on Route 2 and then turn onto Rindge Avenue. I have to warn you about Mellie. She's, uh, I guess the easiest way to say it is that she's simpleminded." Was I quoting Francie? Who cared? "Very sweet. But you ought to know what to expect, not that I know exactly . . ." I went on.

Eventually, as I was taking a breath, Grant said, "Do you ever shut up?"

"Seldom," I said in a tone intended to praise the dogs for the silence they were maintaining. Roy had stopped wailing, and the radio was now playing a song I didn't recognize sung by a man with a range of about five notes. Sammy, unaccustomed to riding loose, leaned against me. "Good boy, pup," I said. "Almost there." We actually were almost there. There'd been almost no traffic. I turned onto Rindge and soon turned left, followed the route to Mellie's, and pulled into her driveway. "This is it," I said unnecessarily.

I tried to make a plan. Grant, with Sammy's lead in one hand and the knife in the other, would get out on the passenger side. I'd be unobserved for a few seconds before I had to follow him. My cell phone was in my purse. But if I turned it on, it would play a little tune that Grant wouldn't miss. With almost no time at all, certainly no time to think, I reached in back of my seat. My fingers found the upper latch on Rowdy's crate. I undid the top latch and quickly undid the bottom one. Then I got out of the van and reluctantly shut the door. Loose in the van, Rowdy just might attract attention. If he heard sirens, he might deliver ear-shattering howls that would prompt the neighbors to investigate or, with luck, to call the police. If I'd left the passenger door open, Rowdy would've been free, of course, but he could've used his freedom to end up on Rindge Avenue or even on Route 2, where he could so easily have been hit and killed by a car. I simply *could* not bring myself to take the chance.

CHAPTER 31

Grant snarled at me to hurry up. His voice was rough and mean, and I felt terrified for Sammy. As I rushed past Grant and Sammy, and up the steps to Mellie's porch, I said, "There's nothing to be gained by frightening Mellie. She's no threat to anyone."

"Always the do-gooder," he said. "Me first. Get out of the way." Instead of ringing the bell, he banged on the door, and when Mellie opened it, he shoved his way in. Stupid of him, really. He should've made sure that he was the one who shut the door. For no specific reason, I didn't quite close the door; it remained unlocked. Leaving the door ever so slightly open was, I guess, an effort to fool myself into thinking that I was leaving something else open, too: my options.

Although Mellie was . . . well, Mellie was herself. She took in this strange man and the knife he held to Sammy's throat, and by the time I actually saw her face, she was in tears.

I struggled to sound calm. "Mellie, we need to do everything this man says."

She replied in that uncontrolled, too-loud voice she sometimes used. "A bad man wants to hurt Strike." Once again, she sounded to me as if she were repeating someone else's words. This time, I knew whose: the words of the woman who'd left Streak in Mellie's care.

Mellie's voice drew Sammy's attention. He tried to move toward me. The most trusting and least protective of dogs, the puppy of our family, the dog we'd babied, Sammy nonetheless felt the urge to position himself between me and any possible harm. I cursed myself for having turned Sammy over to those damned handlers, Teller and that foolish Omar. Sammy knew all too well that I'd transferred responsibility for him to a pair of jerks. With his leash in Grant's hand, he probably viewed Grant as one more Teller or one more Omar; and instead of reacting to the real source of danger, he was responding to the peculiarities of Mellie's speech. Grant yanked Sammy's collar, and the dog looked at me wide-eyed. Sammy wore only a plain rolled-leather buckle collar, not a choke collar, but he was totally unused to leash corrections of any kind. His expression was hurt and baffled.

Enraged and powerless, I met Sammy's eyes and tried to convey a sense of comfort that I didn't feel. Preoccupied with Sammy, I was stunned to hear a new voice, a woman's voice, saying, "What the hell is going on here?" In the doorway to the kitchen and dining area stood Holly Winter. "Take your dirty business elsewhere," she said.

My dirty business? Dog writing? While it was true that articles about canine personal hygiene and, in particular, parasitic diseases occasionally touched on unaesthetic topics, I, at least, always labored to present potentially revolting material in as tasteful a manner as possible. Unfortunately, the desire for clarity and accuracy often conflicted with the laudable desire not to sicken readers. For example, when fresh tapeworm segments cling to an infected dog's perianal area, they honestly do look like grains of rice, whereas once they dry, they resemble sesame seeds, and if you want your readers to be able to check their dogs for tapeworms, you'd better come right out and say so. And if your readers permanently lose their appetites for paella and risotto? If they forever after stick with plain, unadorned hamburger buns? Well, a slightly restricted human diet is a small price to pay for a parasite-free dog, isn't it? Still, aesthetics counts. There's absolutely no need to dwell on such stomach-turning facts as the true nature of the segments — they are sacs of eggs — and their utterly disgusting habit of crawling around. Dog writing as a dirty business? Well, maybe it was.

"This woman has nothing to do with anything," I told Grant. "I have no idea what she's doing here."

"Bringing food for Zachie," Mellie said with great softness and warmth. "Zachie's coming home." Her face was flushed, and her eyes shone.

As if Mellie needed a translator, Holly Winter said, "Zach Ho is on a flight from Heathrow to Logan. The police told me so. I picked up some food for him." Her eyes, too, were shining, and her face, like Mellie's, glowed a rosy red. "And this neighbor of Zach's" — the name intoned with warmth bordering on heat — "saw me and said she had his key. There's ice in the bags, but she offered to let me in." A key on a short chain dangled from her hand.

"So Zachie's milk won't spoil," Mellie said. "He's my good friend." In a gesture that took no more than a micro-second, she reached up and fluffed her hair.

Francie had told me that Zach Ho was one of Mellie's mainstays. I'd had no idea that Mellie had a key to his house, and I was quite sure that the police didn't know about that key, either. I'd been equally oblivious to what might, for all I knew, be a universal female response to Dr. Zach Ho. Now that I thought about it, I remembered that Francie had talked about him with particular affection and indulgence. When she'd said that he had an eye for the ladies, her voice had conveyed not a hint of Cantabrigian feminist blame; on the contrary, she'd sounded titillated. As if to investigate my new hypothesis about Zach Ho, I took another look at Holly Winter, whom I'd have thought incapable of blushing. She was as tiny and bony as ever, but there was something different about her hair. It was still almost painfully short, but brightening its predominant darkness were fine streaks of . . . could it be? Yes! Blond. Zach Ho, I decided, must possess the animal magnetism that Steve unintentionally radiated. Rowdy, I might mention, had that same electric effect on females of his species. In his case, though, the impact was deliberate. Indeed, it was calculated. He had a way of puffing himself up to display his rich coat and massive musculature to greatest advantage, and when circumstances permitted, he'd wait until his female object's eyes were on him to ignore her completely while raising his leg to an impossible height and drenching the nearest tree or fire hydrant in a show of masculine hyperfluidity. So, I wondered about Dr. Ho. The Steve type, inadvertently alluring? Or the Rowdy type, aware of his appeal and eager to show it off?

"I don't give a shit who this is," Grant said. "The toys. And everything else that slut left here. Including Streak."

"Don't use bad words," Mellie told him.

"Screw you," he said. "The toys. And my bitch."

"God is listening to you," Mellie said. "God is everywhere, and God hears everything."

Holly Winter wore one of those boxy linen outfits beloved by academic women, a loose dark skirt with a white shell and a mannish jacket. From the pocket of the jacket she pulled a cell phone. As she flipped it open, Grant dropped his knife to the floor and, as if mimicking Holly Winter, pulled out a small semiautomatic.

Holly Winter pointed a finger at me. "Look what you've done. This is all your fault, you and your dogs with their big stomachs, you and your lucrative family business."

Instead of asking her what she could possibly mean, I ignored her. "We're going to cooperate," I told Grant, who was pressing his pistol to Sammy's beautiful head. "Mellie, go and get everything the girl left here. Strike's toys. Anything else the girl left with you."

"Go ahead and shoot the dog," Holly Winter said. "Good riddance."

"Stay out of it!" I told her. "You have no idea what's going on. All we need to do is give him what he wants. Now stay out of it."

"Traces of methamphetamine were found on the victim's possessions," she said. "Possessions including clothes from L.L.Bean. You're not the only one who talks to the police. L.L.Bean. Maine. The DEA's task force on keeping that very same drug out of Maine. The long border with Canada. The long coastline. The picture of your dog. The *Ellsworth American* is on the Web. Your mother and her marijuana is the least of it."

Again resisting temptation, I restrained myself from pointing out that L.L.Bean ships everywhere and that Gabrielle was, in fact, my stepmother. "Your bitch ran off," I told Grant. "She ran away."

Entirely misinterpreting my use of a technical term for canine females, Holly Winter said, "Ran away? You shot her!" Pointing at Grant, she said, "I've got news for you. While you were busy implanting your drugs in the dogs, your wife here was running around with that redheaded cop the two of you work with."

In desperation, I said, "This is not my husband. This man is not a vet. My husband does not implant drugs in dogs' stomachs. Yes, drug smugglers do it, but I am not one. And I am not having an affair with Kevin Dennehy. Now stop! Mellie, just get the dog toys. And everything else."

Grant moved the pistol away from Sammy's head, pointed it at Mellie, and shouted, "The toys. Like she says. Now!"

The words had barely left his mouth when the front door flew open and in burst a man I'd never seen before. In his hand was a revolver. He was younger than Grant and blessed with the rugged good looks of the young Paul Newman; the breathtaking bone structure, the short, curly brown hair, the irresistible mouth, even the baby blues. The second he spoke, I knew that he was from Down East Maine; you can't miss the accent. "Grant, you son of a bitch, where's Holly? How the hell did you know —"

"Calvin, cool it," Grant said. "I can explain everything."

The name Adam had spoken: Calvin.

"Holly Winter," the statistician said.

"Yeah," the newcomer replied. "Where is she?"

CHAPTER 32

"The little slut took off on me," Grant whined. "Look what she did to me first, Calvin. Waited until I was sick and then beat the shit out of me with a two-by-four, fractured my goddamned skull, and ruptured my spleen. Left me alone in the cabin. I was there for three days before I managed to crawl to the road and get out and get to the hospital. She took off with my money and my merchandise and my blue bitch. But I lucked out. She was stupid enough to take my truck, too."

Mellie looked relieved to understand a piece of what was happening. "The machines come and clean the streets, and I don't like it." Almost reluctantly, she added, "Holly said bad words."

"Her truck was towed?" I asked.

"It was my damn truck," Grant said. "She stole it."

I said, "And the city towed it because that

side of the street was being cleaned. And she couldn't reclaim it because it wasn't hers. So the city sent you a notice that it had been impounded. With the address where the truck was parked."

Grant had had enough. "Calvin, I'm on private, personal business here." He was now aiming his weapon as well as his words at the newcomer. "Get out." He pointed the weapon at Mellie. "And you, lady, I'm telling you, get my stuff, and get it now."

I can sense the beginning of a fight. When the potential combatants are dogs, I do my best to defuse the situation. Now, I decided to make it explode. But I wanted Mellie out of the way. "Mellie, please go get Strike's toys right now. And everything else." As soon as she stepped toward the stairs that began near the front door and ran up to the second floor, before she'd even begun to ascend, I said to Grant, "Look, your buddy Calvin didn't get a notice from the city of Cambridge about an impounded vehicle. He knew where she was. How? She told him. I hate to tell you, but they must've been more than friends. Grant, she didn't just put you in the hospital and dump you. She made plans to get rid of you and start her life all over with everything you had. Your truck, your merchandise, your blue bitch. And your friend, too. Calvin."

"Not to mention my name and my credit," Holly Winter said.

"Who the hell are you?" Calvin demanded.

"Holly Winter," said Mellie from the staircase. "That's everyone. Her and her and the girl."

I wanted Calvin's attention back on Grant. And Grant's on Calvin. I wanted their eyes locked, their hackles up, and their hearts filled with rage. "She was shot," I told Calvin. "She was shot to death with a Smith and Wesson .22/.32 Kit Gun."

I got my explosion. Too enraged to settle for bullets, Calvin hurled himself at Grant and slammed into him so swiftly and so powerfully that Grant didn't stand a chance of using his pistol. He might've done better with the knife he'd abandoned. But maybe not. What Calvin delivered was a full-body blow that must have knocked the wind out of Grant and that certainly knocked him to the floor. Calvin was on top of him as he crashed, and the weight of the two big men made a tremendous boom and shook the little house so hard that you'd have sworn that it had been hit by an earthquake.

But Sammy was free. With his leash trailing after him, he fled toward — damn it! —

the back of the house. Trust a malamute to head for the kitchen. Frozen in terror, Mellie was still on the staircase near the front door. In backing away from the fight, I'd ended up near the couch, the chairs, and the television, which is to say that I had access to the dining and kitchen area at the rear of the house; I could have found Sammy, snatched his leash, and escaped with him out the back door. But what about Mellie? To reach her, I'd need to go in exactly the opposite direction, that is, to the front of the house. If I stepped between the couch and the front window, I'd be near the stairs and the front door; if Mellie didn't spontaneously join me in fleeing, I could grab her by the arm and haul her outside. Calvin was still on top of Grant, but Grant was kicking hard, and Calvin was beginning to look winded. I couldn't see Calvin's revolver, but Grant's weapon lay on the carpet only five or six inches from his right hand. If shooting started, any of us could be hit in the crossfire. Sammy was still out of my range of vision, but he could come bounding back into the living room any second, and I'd have lost the chance to get him out of danger.

The most likely victim was, however, Holly Winter, who had flattened herself against the wall beneath the staircase, only a few feet from the brawl. She was far better positioned than I was to rouse Mellie from her frozen state and take flight through the front door, but she was, if anything, even more paralyzed than Mellie. Her back was to the wall, and her eyes were dark pools of fear. If she'd kept her head, she could have bent down and seized Grant's semi-automatic or at least stretched out a foot and slid it out his reach; she could have helped Mellie; or she could simply have bolted out the door. Instead, she directed all her energy toward squeezing herself against the wall. She looked, and probably felt, as if she were perched on a narrow rock shelf high on a mountain, with her back pressed against the illusory comfort of a cliff and with her feet only an inch or two from a thousand-foot drop to death.

My only weapon was my dog-trainer's voice. "Mellie, go upstairs!" To encourage her, I waved and pointed upward. Mellie looked bewildered, but to my relief, she finally awoke from her trance and began to climb the stairs. Would she have the sense to hide under a bed or take refuge in a closet? I didn't know, but I simply couldn't go after her. "Holly!" I said sharply. "Holly, get out! Go! Run!" I gestured to the front door. Holly Winter remained frozen. Desperate, I picked up one of the bright pillows from the drab brown couch. It was a small pillow and heavier than I'd expected. I took careful aim, and, with the skill I'd learned tossing dumbbells in obedience, hurled the pillow and hit her directly in the face. "Get out!" I ordered her. "Go!"

Grant's fingers inched toward his pistol. Calvin was shouting, "You bastard! You son of a bitch, I'm going to kill you!"

Holly Winter finally left her imaginary rock shelf, descended her mountain of the mind, and bolted through the front door.

Two safe: Mellie and Holly. Two to go: Sammy and me. Feeling my body relax, I was moving toward the kitchen when a patch of bright yellow caught my eye. Veering around, I saw to my horror that Mellie was coming back down the stairs. In her hands was a big yellow gym bag — the bright, eye-catching yellow I'd glimpsed. Tucked under one of her arms was a dog toy, a medium-sized duck that I recognized as a cousin of Pink Piggy's. Damn! Mellie had been repeatedly told to get the dog toys, and, at the worst possible moment, she'd done what she'd been told.

I heard the gunshot while I was still staring at Mellie. The sound reverberated through the little house, and Mellie's immediate and terrified screams seemed to match the pitch of the reverberation and to play hideous variations on the theme of violence. Blood was flowing from Calvin's belly. Grant, struggling to rise, had reclaimed his semiautomatic. From the street, I heard a crash I couldn't identify, not the metallic bang of one car smashing into another, not sirens, not human voices shrieking for help. Hadn't Holly had the sense to summon the police? Or to bang on doors? Hadn't she . . . ?

Grant was upright and aiming the weapon at Mellie. I knew he'd kill her. And Calvin, of course. And me. And Sammy? I knew very little about semiautomatic weapons. The principal fact that had stuck in my brain was that a semiauto held more rounds than a revolver. If Grant started shooting, he might not stop, and he'd have plenty of ammo for all of us.

The front door of the little house shot open, and a roaring mass of gray muscle rocketed in and smashed full speed into Graham Grant, who, for the second time that night, was body-slammed to the floor with such stupendous force that the little house shook. Once again, Grant's pistol dropped from his hand. This time, though, instead of hitting the carpeted floor, Grant's head struck the baseboard of the wall beneath the staircase. All color drained from his face, all but the fading purple and blackish green of his old bruises and the dark traces of those raccoon circles around his eyes.

Sammy! How had Sammy managed to get out the back door, circle around, and enter from the front through the door that Holly had left ajar? How had danger ever registered on Sammy's carefree puppy brain?

I had to act. For all that Grant had the look of death, he could revive. Calvin, too, was comatose, but he might rouse himself. In seconds, I had that semiautomatic in my hand. Covering Grant, I got Calvin's revolver.

Only then, as I rose, did I take a good look at the dog who had saved us. He stood at my left side, his glowing dark eyes on my face. The likeness that had fooled others, the resemblance between father and son, had, for the first time, tricked me. "Rowdy," I said. "My Rowdy. I should have known."

CHAPTER 33

"Her name *was* Holly Winter," said Holly Winter, who had a fleecy pink Ballet Barbie blanket wrapped around her shoulders but was shivering anyway. "I got that much right."

She, Mellie, Rowdy, and I were sitting on the steps of Dr. Zachary Ho's porch. We were in that order, with Rowdy between Mellie and me, and with Mellie serving as a buffer between Holly and, doG forbid, the dog. The Barbie blanket was on loan from a neighborhood child who'd pressed it on Mellie, who, in turn, had insisted on wrapping it around Holly. The EMTs had offered emergency blankets, but Mellie and I had refused them in favor of a couple of old blankets I'd had in Steve's van. The night wasn't all that cold, and we'd been in greater need of soft comfort than of physical warmth. Rowdy gave both. Mellie was snuggled up against him, as was I. Mellie was clutching the crucifix that hung around her neck and a rosary as well. I was clutching Rowdy. Holly Winter had accepted the EMTs' offer but had the emergency blanket clenched in her hands, where it did nothing for her violent trembling.

The narrow street was even more crowded with official vehicles of all kinds than it had been on the day I'd discovered the body of . . . Holly Winter. Ambulances had made screaming departures with Grant and Calvin, who'd both been alive but might get to the hospital DOA for all I knew. I can't say that I particularly cared. All I wanted was to go home, but the gridlock made it impossible to leave in the van, and I had no other way to transport the dogs. Also, I couldn't desert Mellie. Neighbors kept asking her to stay with them, but so far, she was insisting that she wanted to sleep in her own bed. On the topic of neighbors, the sight of so many people milling around and standing in groups, together with the misleadingly festive illumination from the cruisers and the lights of every nearby house, created the impression of a late-evening block party minus the food and fun.

"Shit," Holly said stiffly. "Needless to say, I am very sorry."

"Don't say bad words," Mellie told her.

"There's nothing needless about apologizing," I said. "Apology accepted. Your teeth are chattering. I think you should wrap that emergency blanket around your shoulders. Or I'll get you a regular blanket from my van. Maybe you should go to the hospital. The EMTs offered to take all of us. Or to one of the neighbors' houses. You're shaking."

"It's a normal physiological reaction to stress," she said.

"No one said it was abnormal," I pointed out.

Mellie responded better than I did. With her rosary still in her hand, she put her arm around Holly and said, "Everybody feels sad sometimes. And angry."

"I'll be fine once I understand exactly what happened."

"Now you understand what didn't happen," I said. "That's a start. My husband and my father and my stepmother and I are not engaged in some conspiracy to use dogs as body packers. That's the term. Smuggling drugs in the intestinal tracts of dogs. Or people."

"Drugs are bad," Mellie said.

I said, "But I can see . . . well, some of the pieces you put together are right. Sort of. Maine does have a long history of smuggling. Pirates. Prohibition. But why would anyone use body packers? The border with Canada is mostly wilderness, and the coastline, I happen to know, is three thousand four hundred seventy-eight miles long. I had to memorize that in school. I do come from Maine. You got that right. And Gabrielle, my stepmother, does own a wood lot where someone was growing marijuana. But not Gabrielle. And when you saw me with Kevin Dennehy, you misinterpreted what you were seeing. Kevin is my next-door neighbor."

"The databases —" she began.

"The house belongs to his mother, and the phone is in her name. They live on Appleton Street. You were at my house. You know that it's on the corner of Concord and Appleton. Kevin and I have been friends for years. That's all. And Kevin is the last cop in the world to take bribes or cover anything up."

"The Maine Drug Enforcement Agency is worried about methamphetamine," Holly said.

"Maine's favorite drug is marijuana."

"Maine is considered to be a potentially ideal environment for manufacturing methamphetamine," she said pedantically. "And there's a market. It's mailed from Arizona.

Southern California. That's where Holly Winter was from. Arizona. I talked to her father. He said that Holly was in Maine."

"I heard that Grant was in the Southwest," I said. "They must've met there. They went to Maine. They were dealing drugs. You got that right, too."

"Not really."

"And Calvin was involved. He's from Maine. His accent? Down East. So, Holly obviously found him more attractive than Grant. Who wouldn't? And she put Grant in the hospital and took off with everything he had. His dog, his truck, his money, his meth. And she stayed in touch with Calvin. But you know, in a way, you were right about body packers, except that she didn't use dogs. She used dog toys."

"Strike can't have her toys," Mellie said. "They can make her sick. And don't talk to anybody! A bad man wants to hurt Strike."

"The bad man can't hurt her now," I said. "He can't hurt anyone anymore."

"And she stole my identity because . . . what could be easier than stealing the identity of someone with your own name?"

"She knew who I was," I said. "Grant used to show Alaskan malamutes. He bred them. Then he hit hard times. Drugs. His marriage broke up. He abandoned his dogs. She must have heard about me from Grant."

"His dogs. The least of it," Holly said.

"From your viewpoint maybe. But I think she really loved the dog. If he was a threat to Streak . . . Strike, then maybe that's when she'd had enough. And if they were actually making meth, the environment would've been toxic. The dog could've been poisoned."

"You're very charitable," she said snidely.

We fell silent, mainly because we'd have had to shout to make ourselves heard above the roar of an approaching motorcycle. It wove its way through the jam of cruisers and turned into Mellie's driveway. Even from two houses away, I recognized it immediately: the Harley-Davidson Screamin' Eagle Ultra Classic Electra Glide, the Alaskan malamute of motorcycles, the vehicular twin of my own Rowdy. I recognized Adam immediately. Every light in Mellie's house was on, as were the streetlamps, of course, and porch lights up and down the block. The unnatural brightness and the flashing lights of the cruisers made for a theatrical effect that gave Adam a stronger resemblance than ever to Moses. In this setting, however, he favored Charlton Heston's portrayal more than he did Michelangelo's statue. Since he'd originally been looking for what I now guessed was either methamphetamine or drug money that he'd expected to get from the third Holly Winter, as I guess I'll call her, I couldn't understand why he'd voluntarily entered this macabre street festival, with all its cruisers, its unmarked law-enforcement vehicles, and its uniformed and plainclothes personnel. As I watched, I half expected Adam to hurl a grenade or stage some other kind of violent attack and half expected the police to slap handcuffs on him and confiscate the gorgeous Harley.

Two halves make a whole. Therefore, I was wholly wrong. After conferring with some authoritative types in plain clothes, Adam came striding down the sidewalk. When he reached Dr. Ho's porch, he nodded to me, held out his hand, and said, "Al Papadopoulos. Special agent, U.S. Drug Enforcement Administration. Gabrielle sends her regards."

"Names are so confusing, aren't they?" I said. "I mean, Adam. Or is it Al? What's in a name, anyway? It's hard to remember which is yours, I guess. Unless your name is Holly Winter. In that case, it's easy, since there are so many of us. Our only trouble is keeping track of who's who."

"Just doing my job," said Al. "Sorry. The

278

malamute. The name Holly Winter. Calvin Jones getting a couple of calls from pay phones in Cambridge, Massachusetts. That little misunderstanding about Gabrielle's wood lot. I had to check you out."

"Her name really was Holly Winter." I was still finding the truth hard to grasp. "She didn't borrow mine. That actually was her name."

Holly Winter and the DEA agent spoke simultaneously: "Yes."

"She knew who I was," I said. "Malamutes. Rescue. Where I live. Back there" — I pointed toward Mellie's house — "Grant said that he was sick and that she beat him up and put him in the hospital. She fractured his skull and ruptured his spleen. Or so he said."

"Basilar skull fracture," Al said. "That was the least of what she did. He was in the hospital for four days. Got out a week ago yesterday. Then he was back in. The ruptured spleen didn't show up on the X-rays the first time around, so they missed it."

"Tough cookie," said Holly Winter.

"Which one?" I asked.

"Her," said Holly. "Holly Winter. You, too. QED." She paused. "Which was to be demonstrated."

She had a gift for getting my hackles up.

"I didn't actually require the translation," I said.

"I'm trying to thank you."

"You're welcome," I said.

CHAPTER 34

Mellie clung to her determination to sleep in her own bed. The police told her that she couldn't. Neighbors cajoled. Francie showed up and spoke gently and persistently. We got nowhere until I promised Mellie that if she stayed with me, she could share a room with Rowdy and, if she liked, a second malamute as well. She jumped at the chance. Still, I understood her desire to be at home. I felt the same way, and it seemed to take forever to get there, in part because Kevin Dennehy finally arrived and insisted on hearing everything "straight from the horse's mouth," as he phrased it. I felt insulted. I bear a certain resemblance to the golden retrievers who raised me, but I am not in the least bit horsey. Still, I capitulated, mainly because I felt sorry for Kevin. His efforts to intervene on Jennifer's behalf had failed; the leaders of the social-skills training course had declared themselves unable to *rehabilitate* her. Kevin almost choked on the word. Jennifer's career was in jeopardy. Furthermore, Kevin confessed that his preoccupation with Jennifer's difficulties had had a deleterious effect on his ability to concentrate on his work. Worst of all, as Kevin did not say outright, whereas he considered law enforcement in the city of Cambridge to be his birthright, the case had been taken over by the DEA, the attorney general's office, and various other agencies that were apparently cooperating with one another more happily than they were with Kevin. So, out of sympathy, I told Kevin exactly what had happened. He didn't interrupt. When I'd finished, I said, "And I know you have questions, but they're going to have to wait. I have a lot of questions, too. There's quite a bit that I still don't understand. But I'm exhausted, and I need to get Mellie to my house and settled in, and I need to get the dogs home."

In spite of everyone's good intentions, it was one in the morning when I pulled Steve's van into the driveway. The ride home had been chilly. In liberating himself to come to the rescue, Rowdy had used the back window that I'd left partway open. He had not, as I'd first assumed, simply gone through the glass. Rather, he'd taken out the entire window frame. As I've mentioned, everything in the rattletrap rattled: the engine parts, the frame, the heater, the radio, the doors, and that back window that Steve had had installed when he'd bought the van and had it customized. Kevin had helped me sweep up the glass in Mellie's driveway, and he'd assigned two cruisers the job of escorting us home. The van sounded about the same as usual, and it was actually a good thing that the window frame had been in bad shape. Otherwise, Rowdy could've injured himself in barging through it. He seemed fine.

Sammy, I suspect, felt more than fine. What had he been doing after he'd vanished to the back of Mellie's house? Well, as it turns out — no surprise — he'd discovered the two bags of groceries that Holly Winter had bought for Zachary Ho and had left on Mellie's counter when she was waiting for Mellie to get Dr. Ho's house key. Fortunately, Sammy's booty had been harmless. Indeed, what I'd belatedly realized was Holly's infatuation with Zach Ho had motivated her to buy the best that Loaves and Fishes had to offer: whole-grain bread, organic milk, eggs from free-range hens, Vermont butter, Virginia ham, an array of French cheeses, and other nutritious foods, including, I might mention, sushi and sashimi. On the topic, let me mention something about Dr. Zachary Ho that strikes me as oddly inconsistent, namely, his devotion to the inhabitants of his aquariums and his fondness for sushi. I mean, what is sushi? It's dead fish. I'm crazy about dogs, so you won't catch me . . . Well, enough said. Anyway, even the raw eggs didn't bother Sammy, and his expression clearly said that he felt more than healthy: he felt joyfully triumphant.

As promised, Mellie slept in our guest-room with Rowdy and Kimi for comfort and company. Sammy slept on my bed. Before I fell into an exhaustion-induced coma, I removed the Smith & Wesson from my nightstand, unloaded it, put the ammo in a dresser drawer, replaced the revolver in its case, and shoved the case to the back of the high shelf in the closet. As I fell asleep, I thought of Grant and Calvin. I wondered whether or not they'd make it through the night.

CHAPTER 35

Kevin called in the morning to tell me that Graham Grant had died. I hated to think that Rowdy had contributed to anyone's demise, even Grant's, but Kevin informed me that when Holly Winter — you know which one — beat Grant up with a two-by-four, she inflicted such massive injuries that he'd have survived only if he'd obeyed the instructions of his doctors and taken good care of himself, as he had not. In particular, he should have stayed off his motorcycle instead of riding it all the way from Down East Maine to Cambridge as soon as he was released from the hospital after having his spleen removed. The motorcycle, by the way, was a Harley. The police recovered it from Appleton Street, where Grant had parked it in a permit-only spot. He obviously wasn't a Cambridge resident, and he didn't have a visitor's permit. You'd think he'd have learned about Cambridge parking, wouldn't you? Not that it mattered. The police confiscated the Harley before it was ticketed, and dead men aren't in a position to complain about the draconian nature of Cambridge ticketing and towing. They're the only ones who aren't.

I still didn't understand the chronology until the next day, Thursday, when I went to Zach Ho's house for a debriefing with Al Papadopoulos — which is to say, Moses or Adam or, if Gabrielle had anything to do with it, my honorary cousin-to-be. When Zach Ho called to invite me, he didn't use the word *debriefing;* rather, he talked about the need to impose rationality on emotionally charged life experiences. He also mentioned trauma and healing. I didn't mind. I'm used to Rita, who is a clinical psychologist as well as my tenant and friend, and who is always using words like *catharsis* when all she really means is a good cry. Zach Ho wasn't a shrink, but he was a doctor and a special doctor at that, one who practiced medicine in the third world as well as in Cambridge and one who worked to prevent war as well as to repair the injuries it caused. I knew about him because I'd used Google and some other Web resources. As I've mentioned, a fondness for the Web and for databases was something that Holly the statistician and I had in common. In a way, we'd taken a common approach to researching the identity of the murder victim. The difference was that she'd used databases about human beings, whereas I had delved into a database of Alaskan malamutes. She'd discovered that the victim was actually named Holly Winter. I'd been on the trail of Graham Grant. She'd succeeded where I'd failed, but she'd made the mistake of extrapolating beyond the limits of her data. She, a statistician!

So, as I was saying, Zach Ho invited me to his house. The invitation did not extend to my dogs, even to Rowdy, who was, after all, a hero. Zach apologized and explained. His worst asthma attacks had all been triggered by dogs. As Mellie had failed to mention, whenever he entered her house, he had to take medication beforehand and had to wear a mask while he was there.

"So that's why your, uh, house sitter left her dog with Mellie," I said.

All he said was yes. The topic of his, uh, house sitter was obviously an awkward one for him.

When I arrived in the vicinity of Dr. Ho's house, I took even more care than usual to make sure that I wasn't parking where the city would tow Steve's van. Neither side of the street was due for cleaning, and there obviously wasn't a snow emergency, but around here, you never know what new excuse there'll be to kidnap your vehicle and hold it for ransom: routinely scheduled aerial photography, a march and rally to protest the presence of Thomas the Tank Engine in a local preschool, anything. I was especially eager to avoid drawing attention to the van because I'd done a temporary and probably illegal repair job on Rowdy's window, as I thought of it, with plastic and duct tape, and I didn't want Steve to arrive home to find that his precious rattletrap had been officially declared unfit for the road. It was, in fact, my hope that Rowdy had delivered the coup de grace to the rattletrap and that when Steve discovered that the cost of repairing the window exceeded the value of the van, he'd finally ditch it. But the choice had to be his.

My previous experience with the interior of Zach Ho's house had, of course, consisted of peering through a glass door and seeing Holly Winter's body on the floor of the ransacked kitchen. This time, when I entered through the front door, I felt ridiculously surprised to find myself in the kind of bright, pleasant room that the warm yellow of the exterior and the prosperous neatness of the house and yard should have led me to expect. The fabric blinds visible from the outside let in the late-afternoon light and softened the cold illumination provided by the compact fluorescent bulbs of the lamps. As in Mellie's house, the living room occupied the front, but Zach Ho's living room had bare, shiny hardwood floors and two large aquariums with colorful fish. His furniture was simple and modern, with an emphasis on wood. The couch and chairs were upholstered in terra-cotta canvas, with one wall painted in the same shade and the others in basic academic-community white. Because he traveled to exotic places, I expected to see the kind of travel-trophy artwork that I'd learned never to admire aloud lest I have to listen yet again to "Oh, we found it at a little stall in the marketplace in Nairobi" or "We picked it up on our last trip to Belize" or "It was a special gift from a tribal chief in Senegal." Here, there wasn't so much as a single African mask. It occurred to me that the stripped-down decor might have more to do with Zach Ho's asthma than with his aesthetic preferences.

The beautiful Harley had been squeezed into the parking area next to the bright blue hybrid. Seated on the couch was the man I was still struggling to think of as Al. He wore a light blue button-down shirt and chinos, civilian gear rather than motorcycle-undercover leather, and his dark hair was now as short as Holly Winter's — an L.L.-Bean Moses with a fresh haircut. Holly sat next to him. Little and bony, she looked half his size. She'd softened her boxy beige-linen look by adding a patterned scarf, and she was wearing lipstick that hinted at red. Now that I'd finally seen Zach Ho, I understood his effect on her. Indeed, I understood why the mention of his name made Mellie preen and why he'd succeeded in picking up women at a natural-foods supermarket, of all places. He was gorgeous. No, he was more than gorgeous: he was a Harley-Davidson Screamin' Eagle Ultra Classic Electra Glide in human form. All on their own, my hands flew up and fluffed my hair, and I wished that instead of just substituting cords and a good sweater for my jeans and sweatshirt, I'd worn . . . a dress! Stockings. High heels. That I can't walk in high heels and don't even own a pair bothered me not at all. I could practically feel myself gliding smoothly across Zach Ho's polished hardwood floor in those sexy heels without groaning about the pain in my toes and, miraculously, without tripping. Six feet tall, he had dark hair, dark eyes, and skin of

Polynesian gold. Even when he wasn't speaking, you could practically hear that smooth, powerful Harley engine purring in his chest.

"Thank you for inviting me," I said breathlessly. "I'm, uh, happy to meet you. Hi, Al. Holly. I hope I'm not late."

"I just got here," Al said.

"I can't apologize enough," said Zach Ho. "Everything you've all been through. It's because of my crappy judgment."

"What were you supposed to do?" Holly demanded more sharply than she probably intended. "Cancel your trip to Africa? Renege?"

"No. But . . ."

Al said, "Look, let's fill in some missing pieces here. I'm the one who's in a position to get that started."

"Good," I said. "First of all, who was she? And how did she get mixed up with Grant? And Calvin?"

"Holly Winter. She and Grant met in —"

Holly interrupted him. "Arizona. I reached her father. Holly was living with him, and she met Graham Grant. He was staying in the same trailer park."

"Her name must've rung bells with Grant," I said. "He must've recognized my name. We'd met at a dog show, and I write about dogs."

"What is there to write?" Holly demanded.

"I don't think that you really want me to answer that question." I felt sure that she'd Googled me and knew precisely what I wrote. "The background on Grant is that he was in Illinois, and he got in trouble there. Money, drugs. His marriage broke up, and he took off. He abandoned his dogs. The people who rescued them thought that he'd left all of them, but he actually took one with him. The blue malamute. Streak. And he went to the Southwest. Arizona. Where he met Holly Winter. But how did they end up in Maine?"

"Calvin and Grant were Army buddies," Al said. "But the real reason Grant wanted to go to Maine was business. He'd been shipping methamphetamine there, and he knew there was a market. Or a potential market. In Arizona, he was small-time. The big meth labs were nearby. California, the Southwest, Mexico. Calvin owned a hunting camp he let Grant use. A shack, basically. This is in Washington County, northwest of Machias. He and Holly showed up there last spring. She hated it. That's according to Calvin. He can talk a little. Not for too long at any one time, but he's doing okay. He says she started going to his house to take showers."

"And pretty soon, they were showering together," I said.

"So to speak," Al agreed. "And she used his computer. That's how she knew where to find the two of you." He nodded at Holly and me. "We're looking at the computer now. I'll bet we'll find a long history about you two."

Looking embarrassed, Zach Ho said, "She said she was escaping from an abusive relationship. From what I can tell, she was the one —"

"Not really," Al said. "Grant had made her big promises about getting rich. And all she was getting were trips to the L.L.Bean Outlet in Ellsworth. Wal-Mart."

Holly Winter threw me a look that said, *I told you so.* She hadn't, of course. Her solution to the puzzle had been ridiculous. Still, she'd been right about some of the pieces; she'd just put them together in the wrong way.

"And meanwhile," Al continued, "Grant had set up a little meth lab, and he was dealing, but he still was small-time. That's when he came to our attention. Then he started using. He'd get agitated and paranoid. So Calvin says. As far as we can tell, her main objection was that he wasn't taking care of business. And she liked Calvin better. So the plan was that the two of them would take things over. But she jumped the gun, if you ask me. This is guesswork, but Calvin has a boat, and I'd bet that their plan was to take Grant out and dump him overboard. Nobody'd have missed him."

"But?" I asked.

"Calvin says that Grant hadn't slept for three nights straight. Meth'll do that. And then he got paranoid and went for his dog. The way Calvin tells it, Holly was protecting the dog. If you ask me, she tried to kill Grant. There's no way to prove it, but that was probably the plan all along, and she jumped the gun. I think she left him for dead."

"Exactly when was that?" I asked. "I'm still unclear about the chronology."

"August twenty-eighth. Or thereabouts."

Zach Ho said, "That's when she got to Cambridge. Or that's what she said. It's when I met her. My house sitter had backed out the day before, and I was leaving the next day. We started talking. The problem was the dog. Well, not the dog. I like dogs. The problem was this damned asthma. I couldn't have a dog in the house. Vacuuming and filters won't take care of it. I couldn't have lived here again for months.

But we worked things out with Mellie. She's only two doors away."

Kudos to Zach! He'd managed to get through that part of the story without embarrassing himself and the rest of us.

I said, "You two know each other. You and Holly. When you heard that her name, the woman's name, was Holly Winter, did you say something?"

"I just said that I knew someone else with the same name."

"Any more than that?" Holly asked imperiously.

"No," he said. "Look, I can't say how sorry I am. There's no excuse. Poor judgment doesn't begin to —"

No one spoke up to claim that he'd used great judgment, but Al said that the murder victim had known about the other two Holly Winters before she'd arrived in Cambridge, and I said that since Cambridge is a city that feels like a small town, the chances were excellent that she'd have run into someone who knew one of us, anyway. "After all," I said, "we were the reason she picked Cambridge rather than Boston or somewhere else. She came to Cambridge because of us." Holly Winter probably wanted to say that a piece of trailer trash would've been unlikely to cross paths with any of *her* friends, but she had the sense to keep quiet, possibly because it was precisely what had happened.

Al picked up the story. "So, Zach, you left the next day."

"August twenty-ninth. Tuesday."

"I was still abroad," Holly Winter said. "I didn't get back until September fifth. A week later. So she had a whole week to —"

My strong impulse was to tell her to shut up, but I tried to imagine what Rita would say. "A great deal of what she did is infuriating." I added, "Maybe we need to acknowledge that she betrayed Zach's trust and that she intruded into our lives in ways we didn't deserve."

"Thank you, Holly," Zach said. "Al?"

"So, it wasn't until that Thursday, the thirty-first, that Grant got to the hospital."

"He said that he was alone for three days before he crawled out to the road," I explained.

Al nodded. "He had multiple injuries, including the skull fracture. The hospital kept him until Labor Day. September fourth."

Holly reached into a leather briefcase and extracted a sheaf of papers. The one on top had a gigantic red "No" symbol, a circle with a diagonal line, boldly plastered across a picture of Winnie the Pooh. If Winnie the Pooh was a media character, then Piglet presumably was, too. And if Piglet, what of Pink Piggy? The name was one Steve and I had invented; there were no Pink Piggy movies or TV shows or computer games. Even so, were we arresting Sammy's development and stifling his creativity by giving him a colorful pig invented by Dr. Noy instead of presenting him with off-white fleece balls and other neutral lumps for his fertile mind to transform into creatures of his imagination?

But Holly replaced the media-free material in her briefcase and read from a single sheet of paper. " 'Delayed presentation of a massive sub-capsular haematoma of the spleen,' " she intoned as if the medical report were sacred text. "This is a case report about a man who fell down a manhole. His chest X-ray was normal. He was sent home. Then he developed a painful lump, and three weeks later he was diagnosed with an occult rupture of the spleen."

Zach Ho, who was, after all, a doctor, looked a little perplexed, but I understood. I use the Web to look up diseases and ailments, too. I do it even after Steve has told me what's wrong with the animal I'm worried about or after he's told me that there's nothing wrong except my hypochondria by proxy.

"Thank you, Holly," Al said. "It looks like that's what happened. So, Grant was discharged on Labor Day. Meanwhile, Holly was staying here, and to be on the safe side, she was calling Calvin strictly from pay phones. She was careful. So, Calvin filled her in on Grant, and they were both worried that he'd rat on them or go after her. But she wasn't so careful about the truck."

"I warned her," Zach said.

Al said, "Street cleaning was on August thirty-first. Thursday. On the even side of the street. She couldn't have bailed out the truck without ID. It wasn't her truck. Grant was still in the hospital. He got out the next Monday, Labor Day, and he went home, and the day after that, he got the impound notice."

"With an address," I said. "On this street. Right near here."

"And he went apeshit," Al resumed. "He must've. He was supposed to take it easy, and what he did was jump on his old Harley and beat it to the address on the notice. We don't know exactly what happened then. He found this house. Maybe he looked through windows. When he got in, we don't know what he did first. Tried to get her to

298

tell him where his money was? And the meth she'd taken?"

"And his dog," I said.

"That, too. He tore up the place. And he shot her. In what order, we don't know. Everything was down the street at Mellie's, of course. Cash, meth, all of it packed in those dog toys."

"Shooting her might've been what scared him away," Zach said. "He sounds like a guy who wasn't used to near neighbors. No one heard the shots, but someone could've. That might've occurred to him and sent him running. And there's the ruptured spleen. He must've been in pain. Feeling weak."

"Well, he made it back home," Al said. "Checked himself into the hospital the next day. Had his spleen out. He was there until this past Monday."

"And we know what he did after that," I said. "And Calvin. Holly had been calling him. She must've told him where she was. Then she stopped calling. He was worried."

"Calvin's not a guy who does a lot of reading," Al said. "Basically, none. And a low-profile murder in Massachusetts doesn't make the TV news in Washington County, Maine."

I asked, "But why did they show up at

almost the same time?"

"They didn't," Al said. "Calvin had been hanging around since Sunday, staying at a motel out on Soldiers Field Road. He thought she might've gone somewhere, and he kept checking to see if she'd come back. He must've heard Grant's voice. Grant was shouting at Mellie just before Calvin came in."

"Mellie," Zach said. "The worst thing I've done is to get her involved in this mess."

I feel compelled to leap beyond the narrative moment to comment that one of the things I liked about Zach Ho was his guilt, which was somewhat justified. Despite his peculiar attachment patterns or sexual oddities or whatever you want to call them, I liked and admired him and wanted him for a friend. As it turns out, Steve and I have had dinner with him a few times, not at our dog-saturated, asthma-triggering house, but once at his place and once in a restaurant. Holly Winter has not accompanied us; Zach has no interest in her. I have been thinking about introducing Zach and Rita to each other, but I haven't done it yet, mainly because I can't decide whether to try fixing them up or whether to send him to her for therapy.

"Zach, please stop blaming yourself," I

said and added somewhat mendaciously, "If you think about it, it's really the city that's responsible. If it weren't for this draconian policy about towing and impounding cars, Grant wouldn't have known where Holly was. And Mellie is doing okay. If she'd told the full truth to begin with, we'd all have known what was going on. Not that that's a reasonable expectation. She did what she thought was right. She sees things in black and white. She promised Holly not to tell anything to anyone, and she kept her promise. Yes, she was terrified, but we all were."

"You less than others," Holly Winter said.

"I was petrified," I said. "But Mellie is recovering. She has wonderful friends, and she has her religion. And I'm helping her to look for a new dog."

"The husky?" Zach Ho asked.

"Malamute," I said reflexively. "No, it's the wrong breed for Mellie."

Maybe another Boston terrier, like Lily. Or a pug. A Border terrier? A mini poodle was an excellent possibility. Or a bichon, like Gabrielle's Molly. Gabrielle might know a good breeder with a retired show dog in need of a pet home. Or possibly a mixed-breed dog, a medium-sized terrier cross? Or a sheltie! Yes, a sheltie or a sheltie mix with bright eyes and a lively personality. Mellie would enjoy the ritual of daily brushing, and she'd have fun with a dog who'd like learning tricks. My spirits rose. Until then, I'd found the debriefing informative but depressing. In particular, it was sad to realize that Zach was barred by asthma from the life-affirming experience of owning a dog and had to settle for tropical fish. As to his "eye for the ladies," to use Francie's phrase, I thought that his habit of picking up strange women in a health-food market placed him more in Rita's territory than in mine; in other words, I thought he was crazy. Here he was, a gorgeous, intelligent doctor who devoted himself to helping desperately needy people in third world countries. And his sex life consisted of one-night stands with sushi eaters? And then there was Holly Winter, whose efforts to attract him consisted of softening her appearance without . . . well, I'm doomed to sound like Rita, here: Holly had softened her appearance while leaving the inner person frozen and sharp. But the prospect of finding just the right dog for Mellie? I was elated. Francie had told me that Mellie had special needs. Francie had been right. Mellie's special needs included the best special need of all: the urgent need for the right dog. For someone else with that need,

Streak was waiting. Interested? Visit www .malamuterescue.org. That's the Web site of the Alaskan Malamute Assistance League. It has links to our affiliates all over the United States. Maybe one of them has a dog who is waiting for *you.*

"If you'll excuse me," I said, "I'd better be going. There are some phone calls I have to make. Things I have to do. Zach, thank you for having us here. This actually has been a healing experience."

CHAPTER 36

On Saturday afternoon at three thirty, Steve called me on his cell phone. This time, he had no trouble reaching me. He was on the Mass. Pike, only a half hour from home. I felt like a teenager waiting for a boy she has a crush on. I'd cleaned the house, filled the cupboards and refrigerator with food, moved the van so that the ruined window faced away from our house, brushed the dogs, taken a shower, dried my hair, applied a little makeup, and put on good clothes — not a dress and certainly not high heels, but clean jeans that fit well and a heavy cotton sweater with happy colors and a pattern that suited me. As a matter of fact, it had come from L.L.Bean. Actually, from the Bean's outlet in Ellsworth, Maine. So, I did have a few things in common with the Holly who'd been murdered. L.L.Bean. The love of dogs. She had not been an admirable person, but she had loved a dog, a malamute, a member of my own breed. Therefore, she had redeemed herself.

And the living Holly? The *other?* Eager to welcome Steve home, I took Rowdy, Kimi, and Sammy out to the yard. I'd intended to spend the time planning how to tell Steve about everything that had happened in his absence. I'd thought about telling him on the phone, but I'd decided to wait for his return. As it was, as Rowdy, Kimi, Sammy, and I awaited the man we loved, I found myself diverted by the sudden recollection of my image of Holly Winter as a person trapped on a narrow rock ledge, a person inaccessible and paralyzed by fear. And I finally understood who she was and, in a new way, who I am. She was who I might have become if it weren't for my special need. Yes, there but for the grace of dogs was this Holly Winter.

The dogs recognized the sound of the car before I even heard the engine, and by the time I was unlocking the gate to the driveway, the air was ringing with Rowdy's basso profundo, Sammy's alto, and Kimi's spine-tingling contralto. I slipped out, closed the gate, and heard Lady's excited whines and India's big-girl woofs. Steve was tan and bug-bitten and infinitely desirable. He was wonderfully mine. He surrounded me with his arms and his warmth, and I buried my head in his chest.

Over the caroling of the dogs, he said, "You look beautiful. I've missed you so much. Is everything okay?"

"Everything is fine. Except . . . there was a slight, uh, accident involving your van."

He laughed. "How slight?"

"Not very. Rowdy went through that rear window that's been rattling."

"What was he doing loose in the van?"

"It's a long story," I said. "I'll tell you all about it."

And now I have.

ABOUT THE AUTHOR

Susan Conant is a three-time recipient of the Maxwell Award for Fiction Writing given by the Dog Writers Association of America. She lives in Newton, Massachusetts, with her husband, two cats, and two Alaskan malamutes.

Visit her Web site at www.ConantPark.com